The
Tail of
Emily
Windsnap

The Tail of Emily Windsnap

LIZ KESSLER

illustrations by Sarah Gibb

CANDLEWICK PRESS
CAMBRIDGE, MASSACHUSETTS

Text copyright © 2003 by Liz Kessler
Illustrations copyright © 2003 by Sarah Gibb

First published in Great Britain in 2003
by Orion Children's Books
a division of the Orion Publishing Group

Published by arrangement with Orion Children's Books

First U.S. paperback edition 2006

The Library of Congress has cataloged the hardcover edition as follows:
Kessler, Liz.
The tail of Emily Windsnap / by Liz Kessler ;
illustrated by Sarah Gibb. — 1st U.S. ed.
p.   cm.
Summary: After finally convincing her mother that she should take swimming lessons, twelve-year-old Emily discovers a terrible and wonderful secret about herself that opens up a whole new world.
ISBN 978-0-7636-2483-5 (hardcover)
[1. Mermaids—Fiction. 2. Swimming—Fiction. 3. Houseboats—Fiction. 4. Neptune (Roman deity)—Fiction.]   I. Gibb, Sarah, ill. II. Title.
PZ7.K4842Tai 2004
[Fic]—dc22   2003065284

ISBN 978-0-7636-2811-6 (paperback)

8 10 9

Printed in the United States of America

This book was typeset in Bembo.

Candlewick Press
2067 Massachusetts Avenue
Cambridge, Massachusetts 02140

visit us at www.candlewick.com

For Frankie, Lucy, and Emily
And for Dad

Come, dear children, let us away;
Down and away below.
Now my brothers call from the bay;
Now the great winds shoreward blow;
Now the salt tides seaward flow;
Now the wild white horses play,
Champ and chafe and toss in the spray.
Children dear, let us away.
This way, this way!

from "The Forsaken Merman,"
by Matthew Arnold

Chapter One

*C*an you keep a secret?

Everybody has secrets, of course, but mine's different, and it's kind of weird. Sometimes I even have nightmares that people will find out about it and lock me up in a zoo or a scientist's laboratory.

It all started in seventh-grade swim class, on the first Wednesday afternoon at my new school. I was really looking forward to it. Mom hates swimming, and she always used to change the subject when I asked her why I couldn't learn.

"But we live on a boat!" I'd say (we actually do). "We're surrounded by water!"

"You're not getting me in that water," she'd reply. "Just look at all the pollution. You know what it's like when the day cruises have been through here. Now stop arguing, and come and help me with the vegetables."

She had kept me out of swimming lessons all the way through grade school, saying it was unhealthy. "All those bodies mixing in the same water." She'd shudder. "That's not for *us,* thank you very much."

And each time I asked her , that would be that: End of Discussion. But the summer before I started middle school, I finally wore her down. "All right, all right," she sighed. "I give in. Just don't start trying to get me in there with you."

I'd never been in the ocean. I'd never even had a bath. Hey, I'm not dirty or anything—I do take a shower every night. But there isn't enough room for a bathtub on the boat, so never in my life had I been totally *immersed* in water.

Until the first Wednesday afternoon of seventh grade.

Mom bought me a special new bag to carry my new bathing suit and towel. On the side, it had a picture of a woman doing the crawl. I looked at the picture and dreamed about winning Olympic races with a striped racing suit and blue goggles just like hers.

Only it didn't happen quite like that.

When we got to the pool, a man with a whistle and white shorts and a red T-shirt told the girls to go change in one room and the boys in the other.

I changed quickly in the corner. I didn't want anyone to see my skinny body. My legs are like sticks, and they're usually covered in scabs and bruises from getting on and off *The King of the Sea*. That's our boat. I admit it's kind of a fancy name for a little houseboat with moldy ropes, peeling paint, and beds the width of a ruler. . . . Anyway. We usually just call it *King*.

Julia Cross smiled at me as she put her clothes in her locker. "I like your suit," she said. It's just plain black with a white stripe across the middle.

"I like your cap," I said, and smiled back as she squashed her hair into her tight, pink swimming cap. I squeezed my ponytail into mine. I usually wear my hair loose; Mom made me put it in a scrunchie today. My hair is mousy brown and used to be short, but I'm growing it out right now. It's a bit longer than shoulder length so far.

Julia and I sit next to each other sometimes. We're not best friends. Sharon Matterson used to be my best friend, but she went to St. Mary's. I'm at Bright-port Junior High. Julia's the only person here that I might want to be best friends with. But I think she really wants to be best friends with Mandy Rushton. They hang out together between classes.

3

I don't mind. Not really. Except when I can't find my way to the cafeteria — or to some of the classes. At those moments, it might be nice to have someone to get lost with. Brightport Junior High is about ten times bigger than my elementary school. It's like an enormous maze, with millions of boys and girls who all seem to know what they're doing.

"You coming, Julia?" Mandy Rushton stood between us with her back to me. She gave me a quick look over her shoulder, then whispered something in Julia's ear and laughed. Julia didn't look up as they passed me.

Mandy lives on the pier, like me, only not on a boat. Her parents run the video arcade, and they've got an apartment above it. We used to be pretty good friends until last year. That's when I accidentally told my mom — who told Mandy's mom — that Mandy had showed me how to win free games on the Pin-Wizard machine. I didn't *mean* to get her in trouble but — well, let's just say I'm not exactly welcome in the arcade anymore. In fact, she hasn't spoken to me since.

And now we've ended up in the same swim class at Brightport Junior High. Fabulous. As if starting a new school the size of a city isn't bad enough.

I finished getting ready and hurried out.

"Okay, listen up, 7C," the man with the whistle said. He told us to call him Bob. "Any of you kids totally confident to swim on your own?"

"Of course we can—we're not babies!" Mandy sneered under her breath.

Bob turned to face her. "Okay, then. Do you want to start us off? Let's see what you can do."

Mandy stepped toward the pool. She stuck her thumb in her mouth. "Ooh, look at me. I'm a baby. I can't swim!" Then she dropped herself sideways into the water. Her thumb still in her mouth, she pretended to keep slipping under as she did this really over-the-top doggy paddle across the pool.

Half the class was in hysterics by the time she reached the end.

Bob wasn't. His face had reddened. "Do you think that's funny? Get out! NOW!" he shouted. Mandy pulled herself out and grinned as she bowed to the class.

"That was completely out of order," Bob said as he handed her a towel. "Now I'm afraid you get to sit on the side and watch the others."

"What?" Mandy stopped grinning. "That's not fair! What did I do?"

Bob turned his back on her. "We'll start again. Who's happy to swim confidently *and* sensibly?"

About three-fourths of the class raised their hands. I was desperate to get in the pool but didn't dare put mine up. Not after that.

"All right." Bob nodded at them. "You can get in if you want—but walk down to the shallow end."

He turned to the rest of us. We were lined up shivering by the side of the pool. "You guys will be with me. Let's go grab some kickboards."

After he turned his head away, I snuck in with the group making their way down to the shallow end. I'd never swum before, so I shouldn't have, but I couldn't help myself. I just knew I could do it. And the water looked *so* beautiful lying there, still and calm, as though it were holding its breath, waiting for someone to jump in and set it alive with splashes and ripples.

There were five big steps that led gradually into the water. I stepped onto the first one, and warm water tickled over my toes. Another step and the water wobbled over my knees. Two more, then I pushed myself into the water.

I ducked my head under, reaching wide with my arms. As I held my breath and swam deeper, the silence of the water surrounded me and called to me, drawing my body through its creamy calm. It was as if I'd found a new home.

"Now THAT is more like it!" Bob shouted when I came up for air. "You're a natural!"

Then he turned back to the others, who were squinting and staring at me with open mouths. Mandy's eyes fired hatred at me as Bob said, "That's what I'd like to see you *all* doing by the end of the term."

But then it happened.

One minute, I was skimming along like a flying fish. The next, my legs suddenly seized up. It felt as though somebody had glued my thighs together and strapped a splint on my shins! I tried to smile up at the teacher as I paddled to the side, but my legs had turned to a block of stone. I couldn't feel my knees, my feet, my toes. *What was happening?*

A second later, and I almost went under completely. I screamed, getting a mouthful of water. Bob shouted to everyone to stay put and dove in, in his shorts and T-shirt, and swam over to me.

"It's my legs," I gasped. "I can't feel them!"

He cupped my chin in his big hand and began a powerful backstroke to bring us back over to the side. "Don't worry," he said. "It's just a cramp. Happens to everyone."

We reached the big steps at the side of the pool and climbed onto the top one. As soon as I was halfway out of the water, the weird feeling started to go away.

"Let's have a look at those legs." Bob lifted me up onto the side of the pool. "Can you lift your left one?" I did.

"And your right?" Easy.

"Any pain?"

"It's gone now," I said.

"Just a cramp, then. Why don't you rest here for a few minutes? Get in again when you're ready?"

I nodded, and he went back to the others.

But the truth was, I'd felt something that he hadn't

seen. And I'd seen something he hadn't felt. And I didn't have a *clue* what it was, but I knew one thing for sure — you wouldn't get me back in that pool for a million dollars.

I sat by the side for a long time. Eventually the whole rest of the class got in and started splashing around. Even Mandy was allowed back in. But I didn't want to sit too near those guys in case I got splashed and *it* happened again. I was even nervous when I went home after school — what if I fell off the pier and into the sea?

The boat docks are all along one side of the pier. There are three other boats besides *King* tied up at ours: one seriously done-up white speedboat and a couple of bigger yachts. None of the other boats has people living on it, though.

An old plank of wood stretches across to get you from the dock to the boat. Mom used to carry me over it when I was little, but I've been doing it on my own for ages now. Only just then I somehow couldn't. I called out to Mom.

"I can't get across," I shouted when she came up from below deck.

She had a towel wrapped around her head and a satin robe on. "I'm getting ready for book group."

I stood frozen on the dock. Around me, the boats

melted into a wobbly mass of masts and tackle. I stared at *King*. The mast rocked with the boat, the wooden deck shiny with sea spray. My eyes blurred as I focused on the row of portholes along the side of the boat, the thin metal bar running around the edge. "I'm scared," I said.

So Mom pulled the dressing-gown cord tighter around her waist and reached her skinny arm out to me. "Come on, sweetie, let's go."

When I had made it across, she grabbed me and gave me a hug. "Dingbat," she said, ruffling my hair. Then she went back inside to finish up.

Mom's always going to some group or another. Last year it was yoga; now it's book group. She works at the secondhand bookstore on the promenade, and that's where the group meets. It's pretty cool, actually. At the store, they just opened a café bar where you can get thick milk shakes with pieces of real fruit or big chunks of chocolate chip cookie dough in them. I imagine the book group is just her latest excuse to meet up and gossip with her friends — but at least it keeps her focused on something other than me.

Mystic Millie, who does Palms on the Pier, comes to stay with me when Mom's out. Not that I need a baby-sitter at my age, but Millie's okay. Sometimes she'll practice her reiki or shiatsu massage on me. She even brought her tarot cards once. Apparently they told her that I was about to achieve academic success and win praise from all quarters. The next day, I got the lowest grade in the class on the spelling test and was given three lunchtime detentions to do extra study. But that's Millie for you.

Luckily, Millie's two favorite shows were back-to-back on NBC Wednesdays, so I knew she wouldn't bother me tonight. I wanted to be left alone, because I needed time to think. There were two things I knew for sure. One: I had to figure out what had happened to me in the pool. And two: I needed to get out of swimming lessons before it happened again.

I could hear Mom belting it out all the way from her cabin while I paced up and down in the front room. *"Do ya really love me? Do ya wanna stay?"* She was singing louder than her CD. She always sings when she's getting ready to go out. I don't mind too much — except when she starts doing the video moves. Tonight, I hardly noticed.

I'd already tried asking her right when I got home if I had to go swimming again. She'd gone ballistic. "I hope you're joking," she'd said in that voice that means *she* isn't. "After all the fuss you created, and making me buy you that suit. *No way* are you giving up after only one lesson!"

I paced up to the gas stove in the corner of the saloon. (That's what we call the living room.) I usually get my best ideas when I pace, but nothing was coming to me tonight. I paced past the ratty old sofa with its big orange blanket. Pace, pace, left, right, creak, squeak, think, think. Nothing.

"Better tell me soon, baby. I ain't got all day." Mom's voice warbled out from her room.

I tried extending my pacing to the kitchen. It's called a galley, really. It's got a sink, a tiny fridge, and a countertop that's always covered with empty cartons and bottles. Mom makes us recycle *everything*. The galley's in the middle of the boat, with the main door and a couple of wooden steps opposite. You've got to be careful on those steps when you come in because the bottom one comes loose. I usually jump down from the top one.

I paced through the kitchen and along the corridor that leads to the bathroom and our cabins.

"How do I look?" Mom appeared at the end of the corridor. She was wearing a new pair of Levis and a white T-shirt with BABE in sparkly rhinestone letters across the middle. I wouldn't have minded much except for the fact that she had bought me a similar shirt at the same time she got hers—and it looked a lot better on her!

"Great." A familiar sharp tap on the roof stopped me from saying any more. The side door opened and Mr. Beeston poked his head through. "It's only me," he called, peering around the boat.

Mr. Beeston's the lighthouse keeper. He comes around to see Mom all the time. He gives me the creeps—he looks at you out of the corners of his eyes when he's talking to you. Plus his eyes are different colors: one's blue; one's green. Mom says he probably gets lonely up in the lighthouse, sitting around looking out to sea, switching the light on and off, only having contact with people by radio. She says we have to be friendly to him.

"Oh, Mr. Beeston, I'm just racing out to my book group. We're waiting for Millie to show up. Come in for a sec. I'll walk down the pier with you." Mom disappeared down the corridor to get her coat as he clambered through the door.

"And how are we?" he asked, staring sideways into my eyes. His mouth was crooked like the tie he always wore. His shirt was missing a button, his mouth missing a tooth. I shivered. I wish Mom wouldn't leave me on my own with him.

"Fine, thanks."

He narrowed his eyes, still staring at me. "Good, good."

Thankfully, Millie arrived a minute later, and Mom and Mr. Beeston could leave.

"I won't be late, darling," Mom said, kissing my cheek, then wiping it with her thumb. "There's meatloaf in the oven. Help yourselves."

"Hi, Emily." Millie looked at me intensely for a moment. She always does that. "You're feeling anxious and confused," she said—with alarming accuracy for once. "I can see it in your aura."

Then she swept her black Mystic Millie cape over her shoulder and put the kettle on the stove.

I waved goodbye as Mom and Mr. Beeston headed

down the pier. At the end of it, Mr. Beeston turned left to walk around the bay, back to his lighthouse. The street lamps lining the promenade were already on, pale yellow spots against an orangey-pink sky. Mom turned right and headed toward the bookshop.

I watched until they were out of sight before joining Millie on the sofa. We had our dinner plates on our knees and laughed together at the weatherman when he flubbed his lines. Then her favorite true-crime show started and she shushed me and went all serious.

I had an hour.

I cleared the plates, then rooted through the pen jar, got a sheet of Mom's fanciest purple writing paper from the living-room cupboard, and shut myself in my cabin.

This is what I wrote:

> *Dear Mrs. Partington,*
> *Please can you let Emily skip swimming lessons? We have been to the doctor, and he says she has a bad allergy and MUST NOT go near water. At all. EVER.*
> *Kindest wishes,*
> *Mary Penelope Windsnap*

I pretended to be asleep when I heard Mom come in. She tiptoed into my room, kissed me on the top of my head, and smoothed the hair off my forehead. She always does that. I wish she wouldn't. I hate having my bangs pushed off my forehead, but I stopped myself from pushing them back until she'd gone.

I lay awake for hours. I've got some fluorescent stars and a glow-in-the-dark crescent moon on my ceiling, and I looked up at them, trying to make sense of what had happened.

Actually, all I really wanted to think about was the silkiness of the water as I sliced through it—before everything went wrong. I could still hear its silence pulling me, playing with me as though we shared a secret. But every time I started to lose myself to the feeling of its creamy warmth on my skin, Mandy's face broke into the picture, glaring at me.

A couple of times I almost fell asleep. Then I suddenly would wake up after drifting into panicky half-dreams—of me inside a huge tank, the class all around me. They were pointing, staring, chanting: "Freak! Freak!"

I could *never* go in the water again!

But the questions wouldn't leave me alone. What had *happened* to me in there? Would it happen again?

And no matter how much I dreaded the idea of putting myself through that terror again, I would never be happy until I knew. More than that, something was simply pulling me back to the water. It was like I didn't have a choice. I HAD to find out—however scary it might be.

By the time I heard Mom's gentle snores coming from her room, I was determined to get to the bottom of it—and before anybody else did, too.

I crept out of bed and slipped into my swimsuit. It was still damp, and I winced and pulled my denim jacket over the top. Then I silently climbed up onto the deck and looked round. The pier was deserted. Along the promenade, guesthouses and shops stood in a silent row of silhouettes against the night sky. It could have been a stage set.

A great big full moon shone a spotlight across the sea. I felt sick as I looked at the plank of wood, stretching across to the dock. *Come on, just a couple of steps.*

I clenched my teeth and my fists—and tiptoed across.

I ran to the pilings at the end of the pier and looked down at the rope ladder stretching beneath me into the darkness of the water. The sea glinted coldly at me; I shivered in reply. Why was I doing this?

I wound my fingers in my hair. I always do that when I'm trying to think, if I don't feel like pacing. And then I pushed the questions and the doubts—and Mandy's sneering face—out of my mind. I had to do it; I had to know the truth.

I buttoned up my jacket. I wasn't getting in there without it on! Holding my breath, I stepped onto the rope ladder and looked out at the deserted pier one last time. I could hear the gentle chatter of halyards clinking against masts as I carefully made my way down into the darkness.

The last step of the rope ladder was still quite a distance from the water because the tide was out. *It's now or never*, I said to myself.

Then, before I had time to think another thought, I pinched my nose between my thumb and forefinger —and jumped.

I landed in the water with a heavy splash and gasped for breath as soon as I came up. At first I couldn't feel anything, except the freezing cold ocean. *What on earth was I doing?*

Then I remembered what I was there for and started kicking my legs. A bit frantically at first. But seconds later, the cold melted away and so did my worries. Instead, a feeling of calm washed over me like the waves. Salt on my lips, hair flat against my head, I darted under the surface, cutting through the water as though I lived there.

And then—*it* happened. I swam straight back to the pier, terrified. *No!* I didn't want this—I'd changed my mind!

I reached out but couldn't get ahold of the ladder. *What had I done?* My legs were joining together again, turning to stone! I gasped and threw my arms around uselessly, clutching at nothing. *Just a cramp, just a cramp*, I told myself, not daring to look as my legs disappeared altogether.

But then, as rapidly as it had started, something changed. I stopped fighting it.

Yeah, so my legs had joined together. And fine, now they had disappeared completely. So what? It was good. It was . . . right.

As soon as I stopped worrying, my arms stopped flailing around everywhere. My head slipped easily below the surface. Suddenly I was an eagle, an airplane, a dolphin — gliding through the water for the sheer pleasure of it.

Okay. This is it. You might have guessed by now, or you might not. It doesn't matter. All that matters is that you promise never to tell anyone:

I had become a mermaid.

Chapter Two

It's not exactly the kind of thing that happens every day, is it? It doesn't happen *at all* to most people. But it happened to me. I was a mermaid. A mermaid! How did it happen? Why? Had I always been one? Would I always be one? Questions filled my head, but I couldn't answer any of them. All I knew was that I'd discovered a whole new part of myself, and nothing I'd ever done in my life had felt so good.

So there I was, swimming like—well, like a fish! And in a way, I *was* a fish. My top half was the same as usual: skinny little arms, my bangs plastered to my forehead with seawater, black Speedo swimsuit, and a very soggy jean jacket.

But then, just below the white line that went across my tummy, I was someone else—something else.

My suit melted away and, instead, I had shiny scales. My legs narrowed into a long, gleaming, purple-and-green tail, waving gracefully as I skimmed along in the water. I have to say that I had never done anything gracefully in my life, so it was kind of a shock! When I flicked my tail above the surface, it flashed an arc of rainbow colors in the moonlight. I could zoom through the water with the tiniest movement, going deeper and deeper with every flick of my tail.

It reminded me of the time we went to World of Water at summer day camp. We were in a tunnel under the water with sea life all around us. It felt as if we were really in the sea. Only now I really was! I could reach out and touch the weeds floating up through the water like upside-down beaded curtains. I could race along with the fat gray fish that were grouped in gangs, weaving around each other and me as though they were dancing.

I laughed with pleasure and a line of bubbles escaped from my mouth, climbing up to the surface.

It seemed as though I'd only been swimming for five minutes when I realized the sky was starting to grow pink. I panicked as a new thought hit me: *What if I couldn't change back?*

But the second I'd pulled myself out of the water, my tail softened. I dangled on the rope ladder and watched, fascinated, as the shiny scales melted away one by one. As my legs returned, they felt odd, like when your mouth goes numb after you've gotten a filling at the dentist.

I wiggled my toes to get rid of the pins and needles in my feet. Then I headed home with a promise to myself that I would be back — soon.

Bob, the swimming instructor, was standing in front of me, talking into a cell phone. I couldn't hear what he was saying. Somebody grabbed my shoulders.

"This the one, is it?" a snarling voice growled behind my ear. Bob nodded.

I tried to wriggle free from the man's clutches, but he was holding my shoulders too firmly. "What do you want?" my voice squeaked from my mouth.

"As if you didn't know," the snarly voice snapped at me. "You're the freak." He shook my shoulders.

"I'm not a freak," I shouted. "I'm not!"

"Stop pretending," a woman's voice replied.

"I'm not pretending." I wriggled under the hands holding my shoulders. "I'm not a freak!"

"Emily, for Pete's sake," the woman's voice said. "I know you're not really asleep."

My eyes snapped open to see Mom's face inches from mine, her hands on my shoulders, shaking me gently. I bolted upright in my bed. "What's happening?"

Mom let go of me. "What's happening, sleepyhead, is that you're going to be late for school. Now get a move on." She parted the curtain in the doorway. "And don't forget to brush your teeth," she said without turning round.

Over breakfast, I tried to remember my dream and the things I'd been shouting. It had felt so real: the capture, the voices. Had I said anything out loud? I didn't dare ask, so I ate in silence.

It was on the third mouthful that things went seriously wrong.

Mom was fussing around as usual, shuffling through the huge pile of papers stuffed behind the mixer. "What did I do with it?"

"What is it this time?"

"My shopping list. I'm sure I put it down here somewhere." She leaned across to a pile of papers on the table. "Aha, here it is."

I looked up in horror as she picked up a piece of paper. Not just any piece of paper. A sheet of purple writing paper!

"NO-O-O-O-O-O!" I yelled, spitting half a mouthful of cereal across the table and leaping forward to grab the paper. Too late. She was unfolding it.

Her eyes narrowed as she scanned the sheet, and I held my breath.

"No, that's not it." Mom started to fold the paper up. I breathed out and swallowed the rest of my mouthful.

But then she opened it again. "Hang on a sec. That's my name there."

"No, no, it's not. It's someone else, it's not you at all!" I snatched at the paper.

Mom kept it gripped tightly and ignored me. "Where are my reading glasses?" They were hanging around her neck—as they usually are when she's looking for them.

"Why don't I just read it to you?" I said in my very best Perfect Daughter voice. But as I was speaking, she found her glasses and put them on. She studied the note.

I tried to edge away from the table but she looked up on my second step. *"Emily?"*

"Hmm?"

She took her glasses off and waved the note in front of my face. "Want to explain this to me?"

"Um, well, hmm, er, let's see now." I examined the note with what I hoped was an I've-never-seen-it-before-in-my-life-but-I'll-see-if-I-can-help kind of expression on my face.

She didn't say anything, and I kept staring at the note, pretending I was reading it. Anything to avoid meeting her eyes while I waited for my lecture.

But then she did something even worse than lecture me. She put the piece of paper down, lifted my chin up with her hand, and said, "I understand, Emily. I know what it's about."

"You do?" I squeaked, terrified.

"All those things you were saying in your sleep about being a freak. I should have realized."

"You should?"

She let go of my chin and shook her head sadly. "I've been an idiot not to realize before now."

"You have?"

Then she took my hand between her palms and said, "You're like me. You're afraid of water."

"I am?" I squealed. Then I cleared my throat and twisted my hair. "I mean, I *am*," I said seriously. "Of course I am! I'm scared of water. That's exactly what it is. That's what all this has been about. Just that, nothing more than—"

"Why didn't you tell me?"

I looked down at my lap and closed my eyes tight, trying, if possible, to squeeze a bit of moisture out of them. "I was ashamed," I said quietly. "I didn't want to let you down."

Mom pressed my hand harder between hers and looked into my eyes. Hers were a bit wet, too. "It's all my fault," she said. "I'm the one who's let *you* down. I stopped you from learning how to swim, and now you've inherited my fear."

"Yes." I nodded sadly. "I suppose I have. But you shouldn't blame yourself. It's okay. I don't mind, seriously."

She let go of my hand and shook her head. "But we live on a boat," she said. "We're surrounded by water."

I almost laughed, but stopped myself when I saw the expression on her face. Then a thought occurred to me. "Mom, why exactly *do* we live on a boat if you're so afraid of water?"

She screwed up her eyes and stared into mine as if she was looking for something. "I don't know," she whispered. "I can't explain it, but it's such a deep feeling—I could *never* leave *King*."

"But it doesn't make any sense. I mean, you're scared of water, and we live on a boat in a beach resort!"

"I know, I know!"

"We're miles from anywhere. Even Nan and Granddad live at the other end of the country."

Mom's face hardened. "Nan and Granddad? What do they have to do with it?"

"I've never even seen them! Two cards a year and that's it."

"I've told you before, Em. They're a long way away. And we're not—we don't get along very well."

"But why not?"

"We had a fight. A long time ago." She laughed nervously. "So long ago, I can't even really remember what it was about."

We sat in silence for a moment. Then Mom got up and looked out of the porthole. "This isn't right; it shouldn't be like this for you," she murmured as she wiped the porthole with her sleeve.

Then she suddenly twirled around so her skirt flowed out around her. "I've got it!" she said. "I know what we'll do."

"Do? What do you mean, *do*? I'll just take the note to school, or you could write one yourself. No one will ever know."

"Of course they will! No, we can't do that."

"Yes, we can. I'll just—"

"Now, Emily, don't start with your arguing. I haven't got the patience for it." Her mouth tightened into a determined line. "I cannot allow you to live your life like this."

"But *you* don't—"

"What I do is my own business," she snapped. "Now please stop answering me back." She paused for a second before opening her address book. "No, there's nothing else to do. You need to conquer your fear."

"What are you going to do?" I fiddled with a button on my blouse.

She turned away from me as she picked up the phone. "I'm going to take you to a hypnotist."

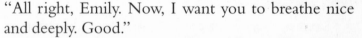

"All right, Emily. Now, I want you to breathe nice and deeply. Good."

I was sitting in an armchair in Mystic Millie's back room. I didn't know she did hypnotism, but according to Sandra Castle, she worked wonders on Charlie Hogg's twitch, and that was good enough for Mom.

"Try to relax," Millie intoned before taking a very loud, deep breath. Mom was sitting in a plastic seat in the corner of the room. She had said she wanted to be there, "just in case." In case of what, she didn't exactly explain.

"You're going to have a little sleep," Millie drawled. "When you wake up, your fear of water will have completely gone. Vanished. Floated away . . ."

I had to stay awake! If I fell into a trance and started babbling about everything, the whole plan would be ruined. Not that I had a plan, as such, but *you* know what I mean. What would Millie think if she found out? What would she do? Visions of nets and cages and scientists' laboratories swam into my mind.

I forced them away.

"Very good," Millie breathed in a husky voice. "Now, I'm going to count down from ten to one. As I do, I'd like you to close your eyes and imagine you are on an escalator, gradually traveling down, lower and lower, deeper and deeper. Make yourself as comfortable as you can."

I shuffled in my seat.

"Ten . . . nine . . . eight . . ." Millie said softly. I closed my eyes and waited nervously for the drowsy feeling to come.

"Seven . . . six . . . five . . ." I pictured myself on an escalator like the one in the mall in town. I was running the wrong way, scrambling up against the downward motion. I waited.

"Four . . . three . . . two . . . You're feeling very drowsy. . . ."

I waited a bit more.

That's when I realized I wasn't feeling drowsy at all. In fact . . .

"One."

I was wide awake! I'd done it—hooray! Millie *was* a phony! The "aura" thing had been a fluke after all!

She didn't say anything for ages, and I was starting to get fidgety when a familiar noise broke the silence. I opened my eyes the tiniest crack to see Mom in the opposite corner—fast asleep and snoring like a horse! I snapped my eyes quickly shut again and fought the urge to giggle.

"Now, visualize yourself next to some water," Millie said in a low voice. "Think about how you feel about the water. Are you scared? What emotions are you experiencing?"

The only thing I was experiencing was a pain in my side from trying not to laugh.

"And now think of somewhere that you have felt safe. Somewhere you felt happy." I pictured myself swimming in the sea. I thought about the way my legs became a beautiful tail and about the feeling of zooming along with the fish. I was on the verge of drifting into a happy dream world of my own when—"Nnnnnuuurrrggggghhhh!"—Mom let out a huge snore that made me jump out of my chair.

I kept my eyes closed tight and pretended I'd jumped in my sleep. Mom shuffled in her chair and whispered, "Sorry."

"Not to worry," Millie whispered back. "She's completely under. Just twitching."

After that, I let my mind drift back to the sea. I

couldn't wait to get out there again. Millie's voice carried on in the background, and Mom soon started snoring softly again. By the time Millie counted from one to seven to wake me up, I was so relieved I hugged her.

"What's that for?" she asked.

"Just a thank-you, for curing my fear," I lied.

She blushed as she slipped Mom's twenty-dollar bill into her purse. "Think nothing of it, pet. It's a labor of love."

Mom was quiet on the way home. Did she know I hadn't been asleep? Did she suspect anything? I didn't dare ask. We made our way through the town's narrow streets down to the promenade. As we waited to cross the road, she pointed to a bench facing oceanside. "Let's go and sit down over there," she said.

"You okay, Mom?" I asked as casually as I could while we sat on the bench. The tide was out, and little pools dotted the ripply sand it had left behind.

She peered out toward the horizon. "I had a dream," she said without turning around. "It felt so real. It was beautiful."

"When? What felt real?"

She looked at me for a second, blinked, and turned back to the sea. "It was out there, somewhere. I can almost feel it."

"Mom, what are you talking about?"

"Promise you won't think I'm crazy."

"Course I won't."

She smiled and ruffled my hair. I smoothed it back down. "When we were at Millie's . . ." She closed her eyes. "I dreamed about a shipwreck, under the water. A huge golden boat with a marble mast. *A ceiling of amber, a pavement of pearl . . .*"

"Huh?"

"It's a line from a poem. I think. I can't remember the rest. . . ." She gazed at the sea. "And the rocks. They weren't like any rocks you've ever seen. They used to glisten every color you could imagine—"

"*Used* to? What do you mean?"

"Did I say that? I mean they did—in my dream. They shone like a rainbow in water. It's just, it felt so real. So familiar . . ." Her voice trailed off, and she gave me a quick sideways look. "But I suppose it's sometimes like that, isn't it? We all have dreams that feel real. I mean, you do. Don't you?"

I was trying to figure out what to say when she started waving. "Oh, look," she said briskly, "there's Mr. Beeston." I glanced up to see him marching toward the pier. He comes around for coffee every Sunday. Three o'clock on the dot. Mom makes coffee; he brings honey buns or doughnuts or bear claws. I usually scarf mine down quickly and leave the two of them alone. I don't know what it is about him. He makes the boat feel smaller, somehow. Darker.

Mom put her fingers in the edges of her mouth and let out a sharp whistle. Mr. Beeston turned around. He smiled awkwardly and gave us a quick wave.

Mom stood up. "Come on. Better get back and put the water on." And before I could ask her anything else, she was marching back to the boat. I had to run to keep up.

Chapter Three

I snuck out again that night. I couldn't keep away. I
swam farther this time. The sea was grimy with
oil and rubbish near the shore, and I wanted to
explore the cleaner, deeper water farther out.

Looking back across the harbor, Brightport looked
so small: a cluster of low buildings, all huddled
around a tiny horseshoe-shaped bay, a lighthouse at
one end, a marina at the other.

A hazy glow hovered over the town. Blurry yellow
street lamps shone, with the occasional white lights
of a car moving along between them.

As I swam around the rocks at the end of the bay,
the water became clearer and softer. It was like
switching from grainy black-and-white film into

color. The fat gray fish were replaced by stripy yellow-and-blue ones with floppy silver tails, long thin green ones with spiky antennae and angry mouths, orange ones with spotted black fins — all darting purposefully around me.

Every now and then, I swam across a shallow sandy stretch. Wispy little sticklike creatures as thin as paper wriggled along beneath me, almost see-through against the sand. Then the water would suddenly get colder and deeper as I went over a rocky part. I swished myself across these carefully. They were covered in prickly black sea urchins, and I wouldn't be thrilled to get one of those stuck on my tail.

Soon the water got warmer again as I came to another shallow part. I was getting tired. I came up for fresh air and realized I was miles from home — farther away than I'd ever been on my own. I tried to flick myself along, but my tail flapped lazily and started to ache. Eventually, I made it to a big, smooth rock with a low shelf. I pulled myself out of the water, my tail resting on some pebbles in the sea. A minute later, it went numb. I wiggled my toes and shivered as I watched my legs come back. That part was still *really* creepy!

Sitting back against a larger rock, I caught my breath. Then I heard something. Like singing, but without words. The wet rocks shimmered in the moonlight, but there was no one around. Had I imagined it? The water lapped against the pebbles, making them jangle as it sucked its breath away from the shore. There it was again — the singing.

Where was it coming from? I clambered up a jagged rock and looked down the other side. That's when I saw her. I rubbed my eyes. Surely it couldn't be . . . but it was! It was a mermaid! A real one! The kind you read about in kids' stories. Long blond hair all the way down her back, which she was brushing while she sang. She was perched on the edge of a rock, shuffling a bit as though she were trying to get comfortable. Her tail was longer and thinner than mine. Silvery green and shimmering in the moonlight, it flapped against the rock as she sang.

She kept singing the same song. When she got to the end, she started again. A couple of times, she was in the middle of a really high part when she stopped and hit her tail with the brush. "Come on, Shona," she said sharply. "Get it right!"

I stared for ages, opening and closing my mouth like a fish. I wanted to talk to her. But what exactly do you say to a singing mermaid perched on a rock in the middle of the night? Funnily enough, I've never had that come up before.

In the end, I coughed gently and she looked up immediately.

"Oh!" she said. She gaped open-mouthed at my legs for a second. And then, with a twist and a splash, she was gone.

I picked my way back down the rocks to the

water's edge. "Wait!" I shouted as she swam away from me. "I really want to talk to you."

She turned in the water and looked back at me suspiciously. "I'm a mermaid, too!" I shouted. Yeah right, with my skinny legs and my Speedo bathing suit — she'd *really* believe that! "Wait, I'll prove it."

I jumped into the water and started swimming toward her. I still had that moment of panic when my legs stuck together and stiffened. But then they relaxed into their new shape, and I relaxed, too, as I swished my tail and sped through the water.

The mermaid was swimming away from me again, faster now. "Hang on," I called. "Watch!" I waited for her to turn around, then dove under and flicked my tail upward. I waved it as high as I could.

When I came back up, she was staring at me as though she couldn't believe what she'd seen. I smiled, but she ducked her head under the water. "Don't go!" I called. But a second later, *her* tail was sticking up. Not twisting around madly like mine did, more as if she were dancing or doing gymnastics. In the moonlight, her tail glinted like diamonds.

When she came back up, I clapped. Or tried to anyway, but I slipped back under when I lifted both arms out and got water up my nose.

She was laughing as she swam toward me. "I haven't seen you before," she said. "How old are you?"

"Twelve."

"Me, too. But you're not at my school, are you?"

"Brightport Junior High," I said. "Just started."

"Oh." She looked worried and moved away from me again.

"What's wrong with that?"

"It's just . . . I haven't heard of it. Is it a mermaid school?'

"You go to a mermaid school?" The idea sounded like something out of a fairy tale, and even though I've *totally* grown out of fairy tales, I had to admit it sounded pretty cool.

She folded her arms—how did she do that without sinking?—and said quite sternly, ."And what's wrong with that? What kind of school do you *expect* me to go to?"

"No, it sounds great!" I said. "I wish I did, too."

I found myself wanting to tell her everything. "I mean. . . I haven't been a mermaid for long. Or I didn't know I was, or something." My words jumbled and tumbled out of me. "I've never even really been in the water, and then when I did get in, it happened and I was scared, but I'm not now and I wish I'd found out years ago."

I looked up to see her staring at me as though I were something from outer space that had washed up on the beach. I stared back and tried folding my arms, too. I found that if I kept flicking my tail a little, I could stay upright. So I flicked and folded and stared for a little while, and she did the same. Then I noticed the side of her mouth flutter a bit and I felt the dimple below my left eye twitching. A second later, we were both laughing like hyenas.

"What are we laughing at?" I said when I managed to catch my breath.

"I don't know!" she answered—and we both burst out laughing again.

"What's your name?" she said once we'd stopped laughing. "I'm Shona Silkfin."

"Emily," I said. "Emily Windsnap."

Shona stopped smiling. "Windsnap? *Really?*"

"Why? What's wrong with that?"

"Nothing—it's just . . ."

"What?"

"No, it's nothing. I thought I'd heard it before, but I guess I couldn't have. I must be thinking of something else. You haven't been around here before, have you?"

I laughed. "A couple weeks ago, I'd never even been swimming in a pool!"

Shona looked serious for a second. "How did you do that thing just now?" she asked.

"What thing?"

"With your tail."

"You mean the handstand? You want me to do it again?"

"No, I mean the other thing." She pointed under the water. "How did you make it change?"

"I don't know. It just happens. When I go in water, my legs kind of disappear."

"I've never seen someone with legs before. Not in real life. I've read about it. What's it like?"

"What's it like having legs?"

Shona nodded.

"Well, it's—it's cool. You can walk, and run. And climb things, or jump or skip."

Shona gazed at me as if I were speaking a foreign language. "You can't do this with legs," she said as she dove under again. This time her tail twisted around and around, faster and faster in an upside-down pirouette. Water spun off as she turned, spraying tiny rainbow arcs over the surface.

"That was fantastic!" I said when she came back up again.

"We've been practicing it in Diving and Dance. We're doing a display at the Inter-Bay competition in a couple of weeks. This is the first time I've been on the squad."

"Diving and Dance? Is that a class you take?" I asked, a wish already forming in my mind.

"Yeah," she went on breathlessly. "But last year, I was in the choir. Mrs. Highwave said that *five* fishermen were seen wandering aimlessly toward the rocks during my solo performance." Shona smiled proudly, her earlier shyness totally vanished. "No one at Shiprock School has *ever* had that many before."

"So that's—that's good, huh?"

"Good? It's great! I want to be a siren when I grow up."

I stared at her. "So all that stuff in fairy tales about mermaids luring fishermen to watery graves—it's all true?"

Shona shrugged. "It's not like we want them to die.

Not necessarily. Usually, we just hypnotize them into changing their ways and then wipe their memories so they move away and forget they saw us."

"Wipe their memories?"

"Usually, yes. It's our best defense. Not everyone knows how to do it. Mainly just sirens and those close to the king. We just use it to stop them from stealing all our fish, or finding out about our world." She leaned in closer. "Sometimes, they fall in love."

"The mermaids and the fishermen?"

Shona nodded excitedly. "There're loads of stories about it. It's *totally* illegal—but so romantic, isn't it?"

"Well, I guess so. Is that why you were singing just now?"

"Oh, that. No, I was practicing for Beauty and Deportment," she said, as if I totally would know what she was talking about. "We've got a test tomorrow, and I can't get my posture right. You have to sit perfectly, tilt your head exactly right, and brush your hair in a hundred smooth strokes. It's a pain in the gills trying to remember everything at once."

She paused, and I guessed it was my turn to say something. "Mmm-hmm, yeah, I know what you mean," I said, hoping I sounded convincing.

"I came in first in last semester's final, but that was just hair brushing. This is the whole package."

"It sounds really tough."

"B and D is my favorite subject," she went on. "I wanted to be seventh-grade hairbrush monitor, but Cynthia Smoothflick got it." She lowered her voice.

"But Mrs. Sharptail told me that if I do well in this test, maybe they'll give it to me in the spring."

What was I meant to say to that?

"You think I'm a goody-goody, don't you?" she said, waching my face. She started to swim away again. "Just like everybody else does."

"No, of course not," I said. "You're . . . you're . . ." I struggled to find the right words. "You're . . . really interesting."

"You're pretty swishy, too," she said, and let herself float back.

"How come you're out in the middle of the night, anyway?" I asked.

"These rocks are the best ones around for B and D, but you can't really come here in the daytime. It's too dangerous." She stuck a thumb out toward the coast. "I usually sneak out on Sunday nights. Or Wednesdays. Mom's always out like a tide by nine o'clock on Sunday. She likes to be fresh for the week ahead. And she has her aquarobics on Wednesdays and always sleeps more soundly after that. Dad sleeps like a whale every night!" Shona laughed. "Anyway, I'm glad I came tonight."

I smiled. "Me, too." The moon had moved around and was shining down on me, a tiny chink missing from its side. "But I have to get going soon," I added, yawning.

Shona frowned. "Are you going to come back some other time?"

"Yeah, I'd like that." She might be a bit strange, but

she was a *mermaid*. The only one I'd ever met. She was like me! "When?"

"Wednesday?"

"Great." I grinned. "And good luck on your test!"

"Thanks!" she shouted. And with a flick of her tail, she was gone.

As I swam around Brightport Harbor in the darkness, the beam from the lighthouse flashed steady rays across the water. I stopped for a moment to watch. Each beam slowly scanned the water before disappearing around the back of the lighthouse. It was almost hypnotic. A large ship silently made its way across the horizon, its silhouette briefly visible with each slow beam of light.

But then I noticed something else. Someone was standing on the rocks at the bottom of the lighthouse. Mr. Beeston! What was he doing? He seemed to be looking out at the horizon, following the ship's progress.

I ducked under the water as another beam came around. What if he'd seen me? I stayed underwater until the light had passed. When I came up again, I looked back at the lighthouse. There was no one there.

And then the light went off. I waited. It didn't come back on.

I tried to imagine what it was like inside. Just Mr. Beeston, all by himself, rattling around in a big empty lighthouse. Footsteps echoing with emptiness whenever he climbed up and down the stone spiral stairs. Sitting alone, looking out at the sea. Watching the light. What kind of a life was that? What kind of a person could live that life? And why hadn't the light come back on?

Dark questions followed me home.

By the time I reached the pier, it was nearly morning. Shivering, I pulled myself up the rope ladder.

I snuck back onto the boat and hung my jacket near the stove. It would be dry by morning. Mom likes the place to be like a sauna at night.

As I crept into bed, I thanked the lucky stars on my ceiling that I'd gotten home with my secret still safe. For now.

Chapter Four

on't forget your things." Mom reached through the side door, holding an object that filled me with dread.

"Oh, yeah." I took my swimming bag from her.

"And get a move on. You don't want to be late, do you?"

"No, of course not." I looked down at the rippled sand between the wooden slats of the dock. "Mom?" I said quietly.

"What, sweetheart?"

"Do I have to go to school?"

"Have to go? Of course you have to go. What crazy idea do you have in your head now?"

"I don't feel well." I clutched my stomach and tried to look like I was in pain.

Mom pulled herself up through the door and crouched on the jetty in front of me. She cupped my chin in her hand and lifted my face to look at hers. I hate it when she does that. The only way I can avoid her eyes is by closing my own, and then I feel like an idiot.

"What is all this about?" she asked. "Is it your new school? Don't you like it?"

"School's fine," I said quickly. "Mostly."

"What is it, then? Is it swimming?"

I tried to move my head away but she held on tight. "No," I lied, looking as far to the side as I could, my head still trapped in her hand.

"I thought we had that all fixed," she said. "Are you worried in case it hasn't worked?"

Why hadn't I thought of that? I couldn't believe how stupid I was! I should have realized that if I let her think I was cured, I'd have to go swimming again!

"I've got a stomachache," I said weakly.

Mom let go of my chin. "Come on, sweet pea, there's nothing wrong with you, and you know it. Now, scoot." She patted my leg and stood up. "You'll be fine," she added, more gently.

"Hmm," I replied, and sloped up the ramp and along the pier to wait by the promenade for the jitney that drops me off near school.

I slunk into homeroom just as Mrs. Partington was closing the attendance book. She looked at her watch and said, "I'll turn a blind eye, just this once."

She always says that. Everyone laughs when she

does because she actually does have a blind eye. It's bright blue, just like her other one, but it doesn't move. It just stares at you, even when she's looking away. It's a bit freaky. You don't know where to look when she's talking to you, so we all try not to get in trouble. She always has the best-behaved class in the school.

I didn't laugh with the others this time, though. I just said, "Sorry," and went to sit down, pushing my hateful swimming bag under the table.

The entire morning was a disaster. I couldn't concentrate at all. In addition to being my homeroom teacher, Mrs. Partington was also my pre-algebra teacher. We were doing some simple equations, and I kept getting x wrong. I was really mad, because I'm good at math, and usually I can solve the bonus questions easily. Mrs. Partington kept giving me sideways looks out of her good eye.

When the bell rang for break, I actually did start to feel sick. Next was swimming. Everyone ran out of the room, but I took ages putting my pens and book away in my backpack.

Mrs. Partington was wiping the board. "Come on, Emily," she said without turning around. "It might be nice to do something on time today."

"Yes, Mrs. Partington," I said, and crawled out of the classroom, reluctantly dragging my swimming bag behind me.

I walked to the gym like a zombie. We were supposed to catch the bus right outside to the Brightport

Community Center, where the pool was. It crossed my mind just to keep walking and not stop at all. I'd gotten as far as the double doors when Philip North called me back. "Oy—teacher's pet!" he yelled. Everyone turned to see who he was talking to.

"Teacher's pet? What are you talking about?"

"Come on, we all saw you showing off last week in the pool. Bob couldn't stop going on about how *amazing* you were and how we should all try and be like *you*."

"Yeah. We all heard what he said." Mandy Rushton came up behind Philip. "And we *saw* you."

I glared at her, speechless. She saw me? Saw *what*? My tail? She couldn't have! It hadn't even formed—*had it*?

"I can't help it," I said eventually.

"Yeah, right. *Showoff,*" Mandy sneered.

"Shut up."

Mr. Bird, the P.E. teacher, showed up then. "All right, break it up. Come on, you guys."

I found a seat on my own. Julia sat across the aisle from me. "Philip is such a pig," she said, putting her bag on her knee. I smiled at her. "He's only jealous because he doesn't know how to swim."

"Thanks, Ju—"

"Move over, Jules." Mandy plonked herself down next to Julia and flashed me a smarmy smile. "Unless you want to sit with *fish girl*."

Julia went red, and I turned to look out of the window as the bus bumped and bounced down the road. Mandy's words swirled around and around in my head as if they were in a cement mixer. *Fish girl?* What did she know?

The bus stopped in the community center parking lot. "You coming?" Julia hung back while Mandy pushed and shoved to the front with the rest.

"In a sec. I'll catch up with you." I pretended to be tying my shoelaces. Maybe I could hide under the seat until everyone came back, then say I'd fainted or fallen over or something.

I could hear chattering outside the window, then it went quiet. A moment later, there was a huge groan, and people were shouting.

"But *sir,* that's not *fair,*" I heard Philip whine. I snuck a quick peek out of the window. Bob was standing there, talking to Mr. Bird. The kids in the class were just milling around; some had thrown their bags on the ground.

Next thing I knew, somebody had gotten back on the bus. I ducked down again and held my breath. But the footsteps came all the way to the back.

"You're not still tying your shoelaces, are you?" It was Julia.

"Huh?" I looked up.

"What are you doing?"

"I'm just—"

"Doesn't matter anyway." She sat down. "Swimming's canceled."

"What?"

"The pool's closed. Budget cuts. They forgot to tell the school."

"You're kidding!"

"Do I look like I'm kidding?"

I looked at her face; she was totally miserable. I stared down at my lap and shook my head. "God, it's just not fair, is it?" I said, trying hard not to grin. "Wonder what they'll make us do instead."

"That's what Mr. Bird's talking about now with Bob. They're going to send us on a nature trail, apparently."

"Duh—boring." I folded my arms, hoping I looked in as much of a huff as Julia. Bob soon turned back toward the building, and Mr. Bird announced with a smile that we were going to Macefin Wood.

Mandy glared at me as she sat down across the aisle. I had to sit on my hands to stop myself from punching the air and shouting, "YES!"

I went to bed really early so I could get a few hours' sleep before sneaking out to meet Shona. I easily found my way to the rocks again and was there first this time. A familiar flick of a tail spreading rainbow

47

droplets over the water soon told me she'd arrived.

"Hello!" I called, waving, as soon as she surfaced.

"Hi!" She waved back. "Come on."

"Where are we going?"

"You'll see." She splashed rainbow water in my face with her tail as she dove under.

We seemed to swim for ages. The water reminded me of those advertisements where they pour a ton of melted chocolate into a bar. Warm, and silky smooth. I felt as if I were melting with it as we swam.

Shona was ahead of me, gliding through the water and glancing back from time to time to check whether I was still there. Every now and then, she'd point to the left or right. I'd follow her hand to see a hundred tiny fish swimming in formation like a gymnastics display, or a yellow piece of seaweed climbing up toward the surface like a sunflower. A line of gray fish swam alongside us for a while—fast, smart, and pinstriped, like city businessmen.

It was only when we stopped and came up for air that I realized we'd been swimming underwater the whole time.

"How did I do that?" I gasped, breathless.

"Do what?" Shona looked puzzled.

I looked back at the rocks. They were tiny pebbles in the distance. "We must have swum a mile."

"Mile and a quarter, actually." Shona looked slightly sheepish. "My dad bought me a splishometer for my last birthday."

48

"A *what?*"

"Sorry, I keep forgetting you haven't been a mermaid very long. A splishometer shows you how far you've swum. I measured the distance from Rainbow Rocks yesterday."

"Rainbow what?"

"You know—where we met."

"Oh, right." I suddenly realized I was out of my depth—in more ways than one.

"I wasn't sure if it would be too far for you, but I really wanted to bring you here."

I looked around. Ocean everywhere. What was so special about this particular spot? "Why here?" I asked. "And anyway, you haven't answered my question. How did we do all that underwater?"

Shona shrugged and tossed her hair. "We're mermaids," she said simply. "Come on, I want to show you something." And with that, she disappeared again, and I dove under the water after her.

The lower we went, the colder the water grew. Fish flashed by in the darkness.

A huge gray bruiser with black dots slid slowly past, its mouth slightly open in a moody frown. Pink jellyfish danced and trampolined around us.

"Look." Shona pointed to our left as a slow-motion tornado of thin black fish came toward us, whirling and spiraling as it passed us by.

I shivered as we swam deeper still. Eventually, Shona grabbed my hand and pointed down. All I could see was what looked like the biggest rug I'd ever seen in my life — made out of seaweed!

"What's that?" I gurgled.

"I'll show you." And with that, Shona pulled me lower. Seaweed slipped and slid along my body, creaking and popping as we swam through it. Where was she taking me?

I was about to tell her that I'd had enough, but then the weeds became thinner. It was as though we'd been stuck in the woods and finally made our way out. Or into a clearing in the center of it, anyway. We'd come to a patch of sand in the middle of the seaweed forest.

"What is it?" I asked.

"What d'you think?"

I looked around me. A huge steel tube lay along the ground; next to it, yards of fishing nets sprawled across the sand, reaching up into the weeds. A couple of old bicycles were propped up on huge rusty springs. "I have absolutely no idea," I said.

"It's like our playground. We're not really meant to come out here. But everyone does."

"Why shouldn't you come here?"

"We're all meant to stick to our own areas — it's too dangerous, otherwise. Too easy to get spotted. And this is really far from where we live." Shona swam over to the tube and disappeared. "Come on," her voice bubbled out from inside it, echoing spook-ily around the clearing.

I followed her into the tube, sliding along the cold

steel to the other end. By the time I came out, Shona was already flipping herself up the fishing net. I scrambled up behind her.

"Like it?" Shona asked when we came back down.

"Yeah, it's wicked."

Shona looked at me blankly. "Wicked?"

"Wicked . . . you know, cool . . ."

"You mean like swishy?"

I laughed, suddenly getting it. "Yeah, I guess so." I looked around me. "Where's all this stuff from?"

"Things fall into the sea — or get thrown away. We make use of it," she said as she pulled herself onto one of the bikes. She perched sideways on it, letting herself sway backward and forward as the spring swung to and fro. "It's nice to have someone to share it with," she added.

I looped my tail over the other one and turned to face her. "What do you mean? What about your friends?"

"Well, I've got *friends*. Just not a *best* friend. I think the others think I'm too busy cramming to be anyone's best friend."

"Well, you do seem to work pretty hard," I said. "I mean, sneaking out at night to study for a test!"

"Yeah, I know. Do you think I'm really dull?"

"Not at all! I think you're . . . I think you're swishy!"

Shona smiled shyly.

"How come there's no one else around?" I asked. "It's kind of creepy."

"It's the middle of the night, gill-brain!"

"Oh, yeah. Of course." I held on to the handlebars as I swayed forward and back on my swing. "It would be cool to meet some other people like us," I said after a while.

"Why don't you, then? You could come to my school!"

"How? You don't have extra lessons in the middle of the night, do you?"

"Come in the day. Come on Saturday."

"Saturday?"

She made a face. "We have school Saturday mornings. Why not come with me this week? I'll tell them you're my long-lost cousin. It'd be evil."

"Evil?"

"Oops—I mean, wicked. Sorry."

I thought about it. Julia actually had invited me over on Saturday. I could easily tell Mom I was going there and then tell Julia I couldn't make it. But I was only just getting to know Julia—she might not ask me again. *Then* who would I have? Apart from Shona. But then again, Shona was a mermaid. She was going to take me to mermaid school! When else would I get a chance to do *that*?

"Okay," I said. "Let's do it!"

"Great! Will your parents mind?"

"You're kidding, aren't you? Nobody knows about my being a mermaid."

"You mean apart from your mom and dad? If you're a mermaid, they must be—"

"I haven't got a dad," I said.

"Oh. Sorry."

"It's okay. I never had one. He left us when I was a baby."

"*Sharks!* How awful."

"Yeah, well, I don't want to know about him anyway. He never even said he was leaving, you know. Just disappeared. Mom's never gotten over it."

Shona didn't reply. She'd gone very still and was just staring at me. "What?" I asked her.

"Your dad left when you were a baby?"

"Yes."

"And you don't know why he went?"

I shook my head.

"Or where?"

"Nope. But after what he did to Mom, he can stay wherever he is, as far as I'm—"

"But what if something happened to him?"

"Like what?"

"Like—like—maybe he got taken away, or he couldn't come back to you or something."

"He left us. And we're fine without him."

"But what if he didn't—"

"Shona! I don't want to talk about it. I haven't got a dad, okay? End of subject." I watched a shoal of long white fish swim across the clearing and disappear into the weeds. Seaweed swayed gently behind them.

"Sorry," Shona said. "Are you still going to come on Saturday?"

I made a face. "If you still want me to."

"Of course I do!" She swung off her bike. "Come on. We need to head back."

We swam silently back to Rainbow Rocks, my head filled with a sadness stirred up by Shona's questions. Of course they were not so different from the ones I'd asked myself a hundred times. Why *had* my dad disappeared? Didn't he love me? Didn't he want me? Was it my fault?

Would I ever, *ever* see him?

Chapter Five

I waved to Mom as I made my way down the pier. "Bye-bye, darling, have a lovely day," she called.

Go back in, go back in, I thought. "Bye!" I smiled back at her. I walked woodenly along the pier, glancing behind me every few seconds. She was smiling and waving every time I looked.

Eventually, she went inside and closed the side door behind her. I continued up to the top of the pier and checked behind me one last time, just to be sure. Then, instead of turning onto the boardwalk, I ran down the steps onto the beach and snuck under the pier. I pulled off my jeans and shoes and shoved them under a rock. I already had my suit on underneath.

I'd never done this in the daytime before. It felt kind of weird. The tide was in, so I only had to creep a short way under the pier. A few people were milling around on the beach, but no one looked my way. What if they did? For a second, I pictured them all pointing at me: "Fish girl! Fish girl!" Laughing, chasing me with a net.

I couldn't do it.

But Shona! And mermaid school! I *had* to do it. I'd swim underwater all the way to Rainbow Rocks. No one would see my tail.

Before I could change my mind, I ran into the freezing cold water. One last look around, then I took a breath and dove — and was on my way.

I made my way to Rainbow Rocks and hung around at the edge of the water, keeping hidden from the shore. A minute later, Shona arrived.

"You're here!" She grinned, and we dipped under. She took me in a new direction, out across Shiprock Bay. When we came to the farthest tip of the bay, Shona turned to me. "Are you ready for this?" she asked.

"Are you joking? I can't wait!"

She flipped herself over and started swimming downward. I copied her moves, scaling the rocks as we swam deeper and deeper.

Shoals of fish darted out from gaps in rocks that I

hadn't even noticed. Sea urchins clung to the sides in thick black crowds. The water grew colder.

And then Shona disappeared.

I flicked my tail and sped down. There was a gap in the rock. A huge hole, in fact. Big enough for a whale to get through! Shona's face appeared from inside.

"Come on," she said with a grin.

"Into the rock?"

She swam back out and grabbed my hand. We went through together. It was a dark tunnel, bending and twisting. Eventually, we turned a corner and a glimmer of light appeared, growing bigger and bigger until eventually we came out of the tunnel. I stared around me, my jaws wide open.

We were in a massive hole in the rock. It must have been the size of a football field. Bigger! Tunnels and caves led off in all directions, around the edges, above us, below. A giant underwater rabbit warren!

Everywhere I looked, people were swimming this way and that. And they all had tails! Merpeople! Hundreds of them! There were mermaids with gold chains around slinky long tails, swimming along with little merchildren. One had a merbaby on her back, the tiniest little pink tail sticking out from under its sling. A group of mermaids clustered outside one passageway, talking and laughing together, bags made from fishing nets on their arms. Three old mermen sat outside a different tunnel, their tails faded and wrinkled, their faces full of lines, and their eyes sparkling as they talked and laughed.

"Welcome to Shiprock—merfolk style!" Shona said.

"Shona, better get a move on. Don't want to be late." A mermaid with her hair in a tall bun appeared beside us. "Five minutes to the bell." Then she flicked her dark green tail and zoomed off ahead.

"That's Mrs. Tailspin," Shona said. "She's my history teacher. We've got her first thing."

We followed her along a tubelike channel in the rock. At the other end, where it opened up again, mergirls and boys were swimming together in groups, swishing tails in a hundred different shades of blue and green and purple and silver as they milled around, waiting for school to start. A group of girls were playing a kind of skipping game with a long piece of ship's rope.

Then a noise like a foghorn surrounded us. Everyone suddenly swam into lines. Boys on one side, girls on the other. Shona pulled me into a line at the far end. "You okay?"

I nodded, still unable to speak as we swam single file down yet another tunnel with the rest of our line.

Everyone began to take their seats on the smooth round rocks that were dotted around the circular room. It reminded me of the three-hundred-and-sixty-degree dome at the Museum of Science movie theater, where they show films of daredevil flights

and crazy downhill skiing. Only this wasn't a film —
it was real!

Shona grabbed an extra rock and pulled it next to
hers. A few of the other girls smiled at me.

"Are you new?" one asked. She was little and
plump with a thick, dark green tail. It shimmered and
sparkled as she spoke.

"She's my cousin," Shona answered for me quickly.
The girl smiled and went to sit on her rock.

The walls were covered with collages made from
shells and seaweed. Light filtered in through tiny
cracks in the ceiling. Then Mrs. Tailspin came in and
we all jumped off our rocks to say good morning.

Shona put her hand up right away. "Is it all right if
my cousin sits in with us, please, ma'am?"

Mrs. Tailspin looked me up and down. "If she's
good."

Then she clapped her hands. "Right, let's get
started. Shipwrecks. Today, we're doing the nine-
teenth century."

Shipwrecks! That beats pre-algebra!

Mrs. Tailspin passed various objects around the
room. "These are all from *The Voyager*," she said as
she passed a huge plank of wood to a girl at the front.
"One of our proudest sinkings."

Proudest sinkings — what did *that* mean?

"Not a huge amount is known for sure about the
wreck of the *The Voyager*, but what we do know is
that a group of mermaids who called themselves the

Siren Sisters were responsible for its great sinking. Through skillful manipulation and careful luring, they managed to distract the entire crew for long enough to bring the great ship down."

Shona passed me a couple of interlocked pieces of chain. I examined them and passed them on.

"Now, the only problem with this sinking was what one or two of the Siren Sisters did. Can anyone think what they might have done?"

Shona thrust her hand in the air.

"Yes, Shona?"

"Ma'am, did they fall in love?"

"Now, how did I know you were going to say that? Ever the romantic, aren't you, Shona?"

A giggle went around the room.

"Well, as a matter of fact, Shona is right," Mrs. Tailspin went on. "Some of these sisters let down the entire operation. Instead of dispersing the crew, they chose to run away with them! Never to be seen again. It's not known whether they attempted to return once they discovered the inevitable disappointments of life ashore. . . ."

I shuffled uncomfortably on my rock.

"Although, as you know," Mrs. Tailspin continued, "Neptune takes a *very* dim view of those who do."

"Who's Neptune?" I whispered to Shona.

"The king," she whispered back. "And you don't want to get on the wrong side of him, believe me! He's got a terrible temper — he makes thunderstorms and typhoons when he gets in a bad mood. Or

60

unleashes sea monsters! But he can calm the roughest seas with a blink. *Very* powerful. And *very* rich, too. He lives in a huge palace, all made of coral and gems and gold—"

"Shona, are you saying anything you'd like to share with the class?" Mrs. Tailspin was looking our way.

"Sorry, ma'am." Shona blushed.

Mrs. Tailspin shook her head. "Now, one rather sorry piece of *The Voyager's* legacy," she went on, "is that it has become somewhat of a symbol for those who choose to follow their Siren Sisters' doomed path. Instances are rare, but merfolk and humans *have* been caught together here. I needn't tell you that the punishments have been harsh. Our prison is home to a number of those traitors who have attempted to endanger our population in this way."

"You have a prison?" I whispered.

"Of course," Shona replied. "Really scary, from the pictures I've seen. A huge labyrinth of caves out beyond the Great Mermer Reef, near Neptune's palace."

I couldn't concentrate for the rest of the morning. What if they found out that I wasn't a real mermaid, and I ended up in that prison?

Shona grabbed me as soon as lessons finished.

"I've had an amazing thought," she said. "Let's go to the shipwreck. Let's find it!"

"What? How?"

"Don't you remember? Mrs. Tailspin told us the exact location. I thought you were daydreaming then!"

She ran her hand along the side of her tail. Then she did this totally weird thing. She put her hand inside her scales. She felt around for a bit, then pulled something out! It looked like a cross between a compass and a calculator. Her scales closed up as she withdrew her hand.

"What was *that*?" I screeched.

"What?" Shona looked baffled.

I pointed to her tail, where her hand had disappeared.

"My pocket?"

"Pocket?"

"Of course. You have pockets."

"In my denim jacket, yeah. Not in my *body*."

"Really? Are you sure?"

I fumbled round the sides of my tail. My hand slipped through a gap. Pockets! I did have them!

Shona held up the object she'd pulled out. "We can find the shipwreck with my splishometer."

I hesitated. It's true that Mom wasn't expecting me home until four o' clock. Should I go?

"Come on, Emily; it must be such a romantic place!"

I thought for a second. "Okay, let's do it—let's go this afternoon!"

Underwater, we made our way slowly out to sea, with Shona checking her splishometer every few yards.

After a while, we came up to look around. A lone line of gulls skimmed the surface. Ahead of us, other sea birds shot into the water like white arrows.

We ducked under again. Rays of sun shone in dusty beams under the water. Moments later, Shona's splishometer beeped. "We're getting close," she breathed as we dove lower.

The sea life was becoming weirder. Something that looked like a peach with tentacles turned slowly around in the water, scanning its surroundings with beady black eyes. Farther down, a see-through jelly-fish bounced away from us — a slow-motion space hopper. A rubbery gold crown floated silently upward. Everywhere I looked, fish that could have passed for cartoon aliens bounced and twirled and spun.

Shona grabbed my arm. "Come on," she said, pointing ahead and swimming away again. Lower and lower, the sea grew darker and darker. As we pressed forward, something came into view. I couldn't make out the shape, but it was surrounded by a hazy, golden light. The eerie light grew stronger as we carried on swimming toward it, and bigger. It was everywhere, all around us. We'd found it! *The Voyager!*

We darted along its length, tracing the row of port-holes all the way from the back end to its pointy front, then swam away again to take it all in. Long and sleek, the ship lay on a tilt in the sand: still, silent, majestic.

"That is so-o-o amazing." My words gurgled away

from me like a speech bubble in a comic strip. It made me laugh, which sent more bubbles floating out of my mouth, up into the darkness.

I couldn't stop staring at the ship. It was like something out of a film — not real life. Especially *my* life! It shone as if it had the sun inside it, as though it were made of gold.

Made of gold? A shipwreck made of gold? A queasy feeling clutched at my insides.

"Shona, the masts —"

"Are you okay?" Shona asked, taking a look at me.

"I need to see a mast!"

Shona pointed up into the darkness again. "Come on."

Neither of us spoke as we skirted around the hundreds of tiny fish pecking away at the ship's sides and swam up to the deck. Yard after yard of wooden slats: some shiny, almost new-looking; others dark and rotting. We swam upward, circling one of the masts, wrapping our tails around it like snakes slithering up a tree, my heart hammering loud and fast.

"What is it?"

"What?"

"What's the mast made of?"

Shona moved back to examine it. "Well, it looks like marble, but that's —"

"Marble? Are you sure?"

A golden boat with a marble mast. No!

I let go of the mast and pushed myself away, scattering a shoal of blue fish as I raced back down to the hull. I had to get away! It wasn't right! It didn't make sense!

"Emily, what's wrong?" Shona was behind me.

"It's — it's —" *What?* What could I say? How could I explain this awful panic inside me? It didn't make sense. I was being ridiculous. It couldn't be — of course it couldn't! I pushed the thought from my mind. Just a coincidence.

"It's nothing," I said, laughing off my unease. "Come on, let's go inside!"

Shona slithered along the hull. Fish nibbled at its sides next to her. I shivered as a silky plant brushed against my arm, swaying with the motion of the sea.

"Found one!" She flapped her tail excitedly.

I slithered over to join her and found myself in front of a broken porthole.

She looked at me for a second, her bright face reflecting the boat's light. "I've never had a real adventure before," she said quietly. Then she disappeared through the empty window. I forced the fear out of my mind. Shona didn't think there was anything to be afraid of. Then I held my arms tight against my sides, flicked the end of my tail, and followed Shona through the porthole.

We were in a narrow corridor. Bits of wallpaper dripped from the ceiling in watery stalactites, swaying with the movement of the sea. Below us, the slanted floor was completely rotten: black and moldy, with random floorboards missing. The walls were lined with plankton.

"Come on." Shona led the way. Long thin fish silently skirted the walls and ceiling. Portholes lined the corridor on our left; doors with paint peeling and cracking all the way down faced them on our right. We tried every one.

"They're all locked," Shona said, wiggling another rotting doorknob and pushing her weight against another stubborn door. Then she raced ahead to the end of the corridor and disappeared. I followed her around the corner. Right in front of our eyes, a white door seemed to be challenging us. It was bigger than the others, shining and glowing, its round brass handle begging to be turned. A big, fat, beady-eyed fish hovered in front of it like a goalie. Shona tossed her head as she leaned forward to try the handle, her hair flowing out in the water. The fish darted away.

The door swung open.

"Swishing heck!" she breathed.

I joined her in the doorway. "Wow!" Bubbles danced out of my mouth as I stared.

It was the grandest room I'd ever seen — and the biggest! Easily as big as a tennis court. At one end, a carpet made out of maroon weeds swayed gently with the sea's rhythm. At the other end was a hard white floor.

"Pearl," Shona said, gliding across its shiny surface.

I swam into a corner and circled one of the golden pillars shining bright light across the room. With every movement, rainbow colors flickered around the walls and ceiling. Bright blue-and-yellow fish danced in the light.

Below huge round windows, benches with velvet seats and high wooden backs lined the walls, large iron tables dotted about in front of them. I picked up a goblet from one of the tables. Golden and heavy, its base was a long skirt, the cup a deep well waiting to be filled with magic.

Above us, a shoal of fish writhed and spun along the yellow ceiling. The ceiling!

"Shona, what's the ceiling made out of?"

She swam up to its surface. "Amber, by the looks of it."

I backed quickly toward the door, flicking my tail as hard as I could. *A ceiling of amber, a pavement of pearl.* No! It couldn't be! It was impossible!

But I couldn't brush away the truth this time.

It was the boat from Mom's dream.

Chapter Six

"Shona, we've got to get out of here!" I pulled at her hand. My fingers shook.

"But don't you want to—"

"We have to get away!"

"What is it?"

"I don't know. Something's not right. *Please,* Shona."

She looked at my face, and for a moment I saw shock—or recognition. "Come on," she said.

We didn't speak as we slithered back down the narrow corridor in silence, Shona following as I raced ahead. I swam in such a panic that I went straight past the broken porthole and almost all the way to the other end of the boat! I turned and was about to start swimming back when Shona tugged at my arm.

"Look," she said, pointing at the floor.

"What?"

"Can't you see?"

I looked closer and noticed a shiny section of wood, newer than the other floorboards, the size of a manhole. It had a handle on it shaped like a giant pair of pliers.

Shona pulled at the trapdoor. "Give me a hand."

"Shona, I've got a really weird feeling about all this. We really have to—"

"Just a quick look. *Please*. Then we'll go—I promise."

Reluctantly, I pulled at the handle with her, flipping my tail to propel myself backward. Seconds later, it creaked open. A swarm of tiny fish darted out from the gap, shimmering in a flash of silver before disappearing down the corridor.

Shona flipped herself upside down and poked her head into the hole, swishing her tail in my face. "What can you see?" I asked.

"It's a tunnel!" Shona flipped back up and grabbed my hand. "Have a look."

"But you said we could—"

"Five minutes." And she disappeared down the hole.

As soon as we got into the tunnel, the golden light virtually disappeared. Just tiny rays peeping through the odd crack. We felt our way along the sides—

which wasn't exactly pleasant. Slimy, rubbery things lined the walls. I decided not to think about what they might be. An occasional fish passed by in the shadows: slow and solitary. The silence seemed to deepen. Inside it, my unease grew and grew. How could it be the same? How *could* it?

"Look!" Shona's voice echoed in front of me.

I peered ahead. We'd reached another door, facing us at the end of the tunnel. "Locked," Shona said quietly. "Hey, but look at—"

Suddenly a luminous fish with huge wide-open jaws sprang out of the darkness, almost swimming into my face.

I screamed and grabbed Shona's arm. "I'm getting out of here!" I burst out, forgetting about the ballroom, the slimy rubbery walls, the trapdoor. All that mattered was getting away from that ship.

We sat on Rainbow Rocks, low down by the water's edge, out of sight from the coast. Water lapped gently against the stones. Shona's tail glistened in the chilly light. Mine had disappeared again, and I rubbed my goosepimply legs dry with my jacket. Shona stared. She obviously found the transformation as weird as I did.

"Do you want to tell me what that was all about?" She broke the silence.

"What?"

"What happened to you back there?"

I threw a pebble into the water and watched the circle around it grow bigger and wider until it disappeared. "I can't.'"

"You don't want to?"

"No, I mean, I really, actually can't! I don't even know what it's about myself."

Shona fell quiet again. "I understand if you don't trust me," she said after a while. "I mean, it's not like I'm your best friend or anything."

"I haven't got a best friend."

"Me, either." Shona smiled a little bit, her tail flapping on the rock as she spoke.

Then we fell quiet again.

"It's not that I don't trust you," I said after a while. "I do. It's just . . . well, you would think I'm crazy."

"Of course I wouldn't. Apart from the fact that you're a human half the time and a mermaid who sneaks out to play at night, I haven't met anyone as normal as you in ages!"

I smiled.

"Come on, try me," she said.

So I did. I told her everything; I told her about the swimming lesson and Mystic Millie and about Mom's dream and the ship being exactly the same. I even told her about seeing Mr. Beeston on my way home that first night. Once I'd started letting things out, I couldn't seem to stop.

When I finished, Shona stared at me without speaking.

"What?"

She looked away.

"What?"

"I don't want to say. You might get mad, like last time."

"What do you mean? Do you know something? You've got to tell me!"

Shona shook her head. "I don't know anything for sure. But do you remember when we first met, and I thought I'd heard your name before?"

"You said you'd got it wrong."

"I know. But I don't think I did."

"You had heard it?"

She nodded. "I think so."

"Where?"

"It was at school."

"At *school*?"

"I think it was in a book. I never knew if it was true, or just an ocean myth. We studied it in history."

"Studied *what* in history?"

Shona paused before saying in a quiet voice, "Illegal marriages."

"Illegal? You mean—"

"Between merpeople and humans."

I tried to take in her words. What was she trying to tell me? That my parents—

"There'll be something in the library at school. Let's go back." Shona slid down off her rock.

"I thought you finished at lunch time on Saturdays."

"There are clubs and practices and stuff in the afternoon. Come on, I'm sure we can find out more."

I slipped into the water and followed her back to mermaid school, my thoughts as tangled as a heap of washed-up fishing nets.

Back through the hole in the rock, back along the caves and tunnels and tubes until we came to the school playground. It was empty.

"This way." Shona pointed to a rocky structure standing on its own, spiral-shaped and full of giant holes and crevices. We swam inside through a thick crack and slithered up through the swirls, coming out into a circular room with jagged rocky edges. A few mergirls and boys sat on mushroom-shaped spongy seats in front of long pieces of scratchy paper that hung from the ceiling. They wound the paper up or down, silently moving their heads from side to side as they examined the sheets.

"What are they doing?" I whispered.

Shona gaped at me. "Reading! What do you think they're doing?"

I shrugged. "Where are the books?"

"It's easier to find stuff on scrolls. Come on. I'll show you where everything's stored." She led me to the opposite side of the room and swam up to the ceiling. We looked through different headings at the top of each scroll: *Shipwrecks, Treasures, Fishermen, Sirens.*

"Sirens—it might be this one," Shona said, pulling on the end of a thick roll. "Give me a hand."

We pulled the scroll down to the floor, hooked it in place on a roller, then wound an old wooden handle around and around, working our way through facts and figures, dates and events. Stories about mermaids luring fishermen into the ocean with songs so beautiful they were almost impossible to hear; of fishermen going mad, throwing themselves into the sea to follow their hearts' desires; mermaids winning praise and riches for their success; ships brought down. We searched the whole scroll. Nothing about illegal marriages.

"We'll never find anything," I said. "I don't even know what we're looking for."

Shona was swimming around above me. "There must be something," she muttered.

"Why is it so illegal, anyway? Why can't people marry who they want?"

"It's the one thing that makes Neptune really angry. Some say it's because he once married a human and then she left him."

"Neptune's married?" I swam up to join her.

"Oh, he's got loads of wives, and hundreds of children! But this one was special, and he's never forgiven her—or the rest of the human race!"

"Shona Silkfin—what are you doing here?" A voice boomed from behind us. We both spun around to see someone swimming toward us. The history teacher!

"Oh, Mrs. Tailspin. I was just, we were—"

"Shona was just trying to help me with my homework," I said with an innocent smile.

"Homework?" Mrs. Tailspin looked at us doubtfully.

"At my school, in—in—"

"Shallowpool," Shona said quickly. "My aunt and uncle live there; that's where she's from."

"And I'm supposed to do a project on illegal marriages," I continued as an idea came to me. Maybe the teacher would know something! After all, Shona did say she heard my name in a history lesson. "Shona said that she'd studied them. She was trying to help me."

Mrs. Tailspin swam down to a mushroomy sponge-seat and beckoned us to do the same. "What do you want to know?"

I paused, glancing at Shona. What *did* I want to know? And—did I want to know at all?

"Emily's doing her project on Shiprock," Shona said, picking up my thread. "That's why she's here. We need to find out if there've been any illegal marriages around here."

"Indeed there has been one," Mrs. Tailspin said, patting the bun on her head. "Rather a well-known incident. Do you remember, Shona? We covered it last term." She frowned. "Or were you too busy day-dreaming at the time?"

"Can you tell me about it?" I asked.

Mrs. Tailspin turned back to me. "Very well."

I tried to keep still on my sponge while I waited for her to carry on.

"A group of humans once found out a little too much about the merfolk world," she began. "There had been a yacht race nearby. A couple of the boats went off course and capsized. Some mermen found them and helped them. They had to have their memories wiped afterward." She paused. "But one was missed."

"And?"

"And she didn't forget. Word spread, both in her world and our own. They started meeting up. Humans and merfolk. At one point, there was talk of them all going off to a desert island to live together. The rumor was that there was even a place where it was already happening."

"*Really?*" Shona said.

"Like I said, it was a rumor. I don't believe for one moment that it existed, or for that matter, exists. But they kept meeting. As I'm sure you can imagine, Neptune was *not* pleased."

"What happened?" I asked.

"There were storms for weeks. He said that if he

76

ever caught anyone consorting with a human, they would be imprisoned for life. He visited every merfolk area personally."

"He hardly ever does that!" Shona said. "He always stays in his main palace, except when he goes on exotic vacations, or visits his other palaces. He's got them all over the world, doesn't he?"

"That's right, Shona."

"So he came to Shiprock?" I asked.

"He did indeed."

Shona bounced off her seat. "Did you meet him?"

Mrs. Tailspin nodded.

"Really? What's he like?"

"Angry, loud, covered in gold—but with a certain charisma."

"Wow!" Shona gazed at Mrs. Tailspin.

"The preparation took weeks," she continued. "As you know, Neptune can become most unhappy if he is not presented with adequate jewels and crystals when he visits. Our menfolk went on daily searches under the rocks. We made him a new scepter as a present."

"Was he pleased?"

"Very. He gave the town a dolphin as a thank-you."

"So, did the meetings stop?" I asked. "Between the merpeople and the humans?"

"Sadly, no. They continued to meet in secret. I don't know how they lived with themselves, defying Neptune like that."

"And the marriage . . . ?" I asked, holding my breath.

"Yes, there was a merman. A poet. Jake. He married one of the women at Rainbow Rocks—"

Something stirred in the back of my mind; thoughts that I couldn't quite grasp, like bubbles that burst as soon as you touch them.

Shona didn't look at me. "What was his last name?" she asked, her voice jagged like the library walls.

Mrs. Tailspin patted her bun again. Tutted. Squinted. "Whirlstand? Whichmap? Wisplatch? No, I can't remember."

Looking down, I closed my eyes. "Was it Windsnap?" I asked.

"Windsnap! Yes, that might have been it."

The bubbles turned to rocks and started clogging up my throat.

"And they had a daughter," she continued. "That was when they were caught."

"When exactly was this?" I managed to squeeze out.

"Let's see . . . twelve or thirteen years ago."

I nodded, not trusting myself to speak.

"Gave themselves away with that. The silly woman brought the child to Rainbow Rocks and that was when we got him."

"Got him? What did they do to him?" Shona asked.

"Prison," Mrs. Tailspin said with a proud smile. "Neptune decided to make an example of him. He said Jake would be locked up for life."

"What about the baby?" I asked, swallowing hard while I waited for her to reply.

"Baby? Goodness knows. But we stopped that one." Mrs. Tailspin smiled again. "That's what you'll be doing when you're a siren, Shona. You'll be as good as that."

Shona reddened. "I haven't completely decided what I want to be yet," she said.

"Very well." Mrs. Tailspin glanced around the room. Mergirls and boys were still reading. Some were talking quietly in groups. "Now, girls, if there's nothing else, I must check on my library group."

"Yes. Thanks," I managed to say. I don't know how.

We sat in silence after she'd gone.

"It's me, isn't it?" I said eventually, staring ahead of me at nothing.

"Do you want it to be?"

"I don't know what I want. I don't even know who I am anymore."

Shona swam in front of me and made me look at her. "Emily, maybe we can find out more. He's still alive! He's out there somewhere!"

"Yeah, in prison. For life."

"But at least he didn't want to leave you!"

Perhaps he still thought about me. Perhaps I *could* find out more.

"I think we should go back to the shipwreck," Shona said.

"*What?* No way!"

"Think about it! Your mom's dream, what Mrs. Tailspin said in the lesson. They might have gone there together!"

Maybe she was right. I didn't have any better ideas. "I'll think about it," I said. "Give me a few days."

"Wednesday, then."

"Okay."

"Look, I'd better be heading back." I slithered over to the spiral tube.

"Will you be all right?"

"Yeah." I tried to smile. Would I? That was anyone's guess.

I swam home through the silent water, my thoughts as crowded and unfathomable as the sea.

Chapter Seven

"Are you eating that or playing with it?" Mom asked over the top of her glasses as I stirred my cereal, watching the milk turn brown and the flakes fade into a soggy beige.

"What? Huh? Oh, sorry." I took a mouthful, then stirred some more.

Mom had the *Times* spread out in front of her. She flicked through the pages, tutting every now and then, or frowning and pushing her glasses farther up her nose.

How was I ever going to find out what was going on? It's not exactly the kind of thing that crops up naturally at Sunday breakfast: "Oh, by the way,

Mom, I've been meaning to ask. I don't suppose you married a merman, had his child, and then never saw him again? OR THOUGHT TO TELL YOUR DAUGHTER ABOUT IT? *HUH???*"

I squelched my cereal against the side of the bowl, splashing milk onto the table.

"Be careful, sweetie." Mom wiped off a splash from the edge of her paper with her hand. Then she looked at me. "Are you all right? It's not like you to ignore your breakfast."

"I'm fine." I got up and emptied my bowl into the sink.

"Emily?"

I ignored her as I sat back down at the table and pulled at my hair, winding it around my fingers.

Mom took her glasses off. That meant it was serious. Then she folded her arms. Double serious. "I'm waiting," she said, her mouth tight, her eyes small. "*Emily,* I said I'm —"

"Why do you never talk about my dad?"

Mom jerked in her seat as though I'd punched her. *"What?"*

"You never talk about my father," I said, my voice coming out quieter this time. "I don't know anything about him. It's as though he never existed."

Mom put her glasses back on; then she took them off again and got up. She turned on one of the gas burners, put the kettle on it, and gazed at the flickering flame. "I don't know what to *say,*" she muttered eventually.

"Why not start by telling me something about him?"

"I want to. Darling, of course I want to."

"So how come you never have?"

Her eyes had gone all watery, and she rubbed them with the sleeve of her sweater. "I don't know. I just can't — I can't do it."

If there's one thing I can't *bear*, it's Mom crying. "Look, it's okay. I'm sorry." I got out of my seat and put my arms around her shoulders. "It doesn't matter."

"But it does." She wiped her nose with the edge of the tablecloth. "I want to tell you. But I can't, I can't, I — "

"It's okay, Mom, honest. You don't have to tell me."

"But I want to," she sobbed. "I just can't remember!"

"You can't remember?" I let go and stared at her. "You don't remember the man you married?"

She looked at me through bloodshot eyes. "Well, yes — no. I mean, sometimes I think I remember things. But then it goes again. Disappears."

"Disappears."

"Just like he did," she said quietly, her body shaking, her head in her hands. "I can't even remember my own husband. Your father. Oh, I'm a terrible mother."

"Don't start that," I sighed. "You're a great mother. The best."

"Really?" She smoothed down her skirt against her lap. I forced myself to smile. She looked up and stroked my cheek with her thumb. "I must have done something right to get you," she said weakly.

I stood up. "Look, just forget it. It doesn't matter. Okay?"

"You deserve better than—"

"Come on, Mom. It's all right," I said firmly. "Hey, I think I'll go over to the arcade, okay?"

She pinched my cheek. "Munchkin," she sniffed. "Pass me my purse."

She handed me two dollars, and I headed up the stairs.

I dawdled as I made my way past the video arcade. Not fair. Nothing was fair. I couldn't even waste a quarter on the Skee-Ball. On top of everything else, I didn't need Mandy turning up and going after me just for being there.

I bought some cotton candy from the end of the pier and wandered down to the boardwalk, my head filled with thoughts and questions. I didn't notice Mr. Beeston coming toward me.

"Watch yourself," he said as I nearly walked into him.

"Sorry. I was miles away."

He smiled at me in that way that always gives me weird shivers in my neck and arms. One side of his mouth turned up, the other reached down, and his crooked teeth poked out through the dark gap in between.

"How's Mom?" he asked.

That's when I had a thought. Mr. Beeston had been around a long time. He was kind of friendly with Mom. Maybe he'd know something.

"She's not doing that great, actually," I said as I took a bite, the pink fluff melting into sugar in my mouth.

"Oh? Why not?"

"She's a bit sad about . . . some things."

"Things? What *things*?" he said quickly, his smile gone.

"Just . . ."

"Is she ill? What's the matter?" Mr. Beeston's face turned hard as he narrowed his eyes at me.

"Well, my father . . ." I pulled at my cotton candy and a long piece came away like a loose thread from a fluffy pink ball of mohair yarn. I folded it over into my mouth.

"Your *what*?" Mr. Beeston burst out. What *was* his problem?

"I was asking her about my father and she got upset."

He lowered his voice. "What did she tell you?"

"She didn't tell me anything."

"Nothing at all?"

"She said she couldn't remember anything. Then she started crying."

"Couldn't remember anything? That's what she said?"

I nodded.

"You're quite sure now? Nothing at all?"

"Yes. Nothing."

"All right, then." Mr. Beeston breathed out hard through his nose. It made a low whistling sound.

"So, I wondered if you could help me," I continued, trying to sound casual.

"Me? How on earth can *I* help you?" he snapped.

"I just wondered if she'd ever talked to you about him. With you being her friend and everything."

He examined my face, squeezing his eyes down to narrow slits as he stared. I wanted to run away. Of course he wouldn't know anything. Why would she talk to him and not me? I tried to hold his eyes but he was staring at me so hard I had to look away.

He took hold of me by my elbow and pointed up the promenade with his other hand. "I think it's time you and I had a little chat," he said.

I tried to shake my elbow away as we walked, but he held it tighter and walked faster. We'd gotten all the way to the end of the boardwalk before he let go and motioned for me to sit down on a bench.

"Now, listen to me and listen well, because I'll tell you this once and once only."

I waited.

"And I don't want you bothering your mother with it afterward. You've upset her enough already."

"But I—"

"Never mind, never mind." He raised his hand to stop me. "You couldn't have known."

He wiped his forehead with a hanky. "Now then," he said, shifting his weight onto his side as he put his hanky away. His trousers had a hole just below the pocket. "Your father and I, we used to be friends. Best friends. Some folks even thought we were brothers; that's how close we were."

Brothers? Surely Mr. Beeston was lots older than my father? I opened my mouth to speak.

"He was like a kid brother to me. We did everything together."

"Like what?"

"What?"

"What things did you do? I want to know what he was like."

"All the things young boys get up to," he snapped. "We went fishing together. Went out on our bikes—"

"Motorbikes?"

"Yes, yes, motorbikes, mountain bikes—all of that. We were best friends. Chased the girls together, too."

Imagining Mr. Beeston chasing girls, I shuddered.

He cleared his throat. "Then, of course, he met your mother and things changed."

"Changed? How?"

"Well, one might say they fell in love. At least, she did. Very much so."

"And what about my dad?"

"He did a very good impression of love, for a while. He certainly didn't want to fool around with cars anymore."

"I thought you said he liked bikes."

"Cars, bikes — whatever. He wasn't interested. They spent all their time together."

Mr. Beeston stared into the distance, his hands in his pockets. He looked as though he was struggling with something. Then he jingled his coins and said, "But of course it didn't last. Your father turned out not to be the gentleman we all had believed he was."

"What do you mean?"

"This is rather a delicate matter. But I shall tell you. Let us say he wasn't the most *responsible* person. He was happy enough to lead your mother up the garden path, but not prepared to stay by her side when they got to the gate."

"Huh?"

His face reddened. "He was content to sow but not reap."

"Mr. Beeston, I don't know what you're talking about."

"Good grief, child. I'm talking about responsibility,"

he snapped. "Where do you think *you* came from?"

"Do you mean he got my mom pregnant with me and then ran off?"

"Yes, yes, that is what I mean."

Why didn't you say so, then? I wanted to say—but didn't dare. Mr. Beeston looked so angry. "So he left her?" I asked, just to make sure I'd got it right.

"Yes, he left her," he replied through tight lips.

"Where did he go?"

"That's just it. No one ever heard from him again. The strain was obviously too much for him," he said sarcastically.

"What strain?"

"Fatherhood. Good-for-nothing slacker. Never willing to grow up and take responsibility." Mr. Beeston looked away. "What he did—it was despicable," he said, his voice becoming raspy. "I will never forgive him." He got up from the bench, his face hard and set. "Never," he repeated. Something about the way he said it made me hope I'd never get on his wrong side.

I followed him as we carried on along the boardwalk. "Didn't anybody try to find him?"

"Find him?" Mr. Beeston looked at me, but it was as though he were seeing right through me. His eyes wouldn't meet mine. "Find him?" he repeated. "Yes—of course we tried. No one could have done more than I did. I traveled around for weeks, put up posters. We even had a message on the radio, begging him to come home and meet his — well, his . . ."

"His daughter?"

Mr. Beeston didn't reply.

"So he never even saw me?"

"We did everything we could."

I looked down the wide boards of the promenade, trying to take in what I'd heard. It *couldn't* be true. Could it? A young couple ambled toward us, the man holding a baby up in the air, the woman laughing, a spaniel jumping up between them. Farther down, an elderly couple were walking slowly against the wind, arms linked.

"I think I need to go now," I said. We'd walked all the way around to the lighthouse.

Mr. Beeston pulled me back by my arm. "You're not to talk to your mother about this, do you hear me?"

"Why not?"

"You saw what happened. It's far too painful for her." He tightened his grip, his fingers biting into my arm. "Promise me you won't mention it."

I didn't say anything.

Mr. Beeston looked hard into my eyes. "People can block things out completely if the memory is too much to cope with. That's a scientific fact. There'll be all sorts of trouble if you try to make her talk about this." He pulled on my arm, his face inches from mine. "And you don't want trouble — do you?" he said in a whisper.

I shook my head.

"*Do* you?" he repeated with another yank on my arm.

"No — of course not," my voice wobbled.

He smiled his wonky smile at me and let go of my arm. "Good," he said. "Good. Now, will I be seeing you when I come over this afternoon?"

"I'm going out," I said quickly. I'd think of something to do. I couldn't cope with Sunday coffee with Mom and Mr. Beeston. Especially now.

"Very well. Tell your mother I'll be over at three o'clock."

"Yeah."

We stood by the lighthouse. For a moment, I had a vision of him throwing me inside and locking me in! Why would he do that? He'd never done anything to hurt me — before today. I rubbed my arm. I could still feel the pinch of his fingers digging into my skin. But it was nothing compared with the disappointment I felt in my chest. Jake wasn't my father, after all, if Mr. Beeston was to be believed. And he had no reason to lie — did he? Nothing made sense anymore.

"Now, let's see, where's the, hmm . . ." Mr. Beeston talked to himself as he fumbled with his keys. He had about five key rings rattling on a long chain. But then he gasped. "What — where's my . . ."

"What's wrong?"

He ignored me. "It can't be missing. It can't be." He felt in his pants pockets, pulling the insides out and shaking out his handkerchief. "It was here. I'm sure it was."

"The lighthouse key?"

"No, not the lighthouse key, the—" He stopped fumbling and looked up at me, as if he'd only just remembered I was there, his eyes dark and hard. "You're still here," he said. "Go on. Leave me alone. But don't forget our chat. It's between you and me. Remember, you don't want to cause any *trouble*." Then he unlocked the lighthouse door. "I've got some important things to do," he said. Squinting into my eyes, he added, "I'll see you again soon." For some reason, it sounded like a threat.

Before I had a chance to say anything else, he'd slipped inside and shut the door behind him. A second later, a bolt slid across.

As I turned to leave, I kicked something up in the dust. It glinted at me. A key ring. I picked it up. There was a brass plate on the ring with crystals around the edges. There was a picture of a pitchfork or something engraved on one side.

Two keys hung from the ring: one big chunky one, the other a little metal one, same as Mom has for our suitcase. A tiny gold chain hung from the plate; a clasp at its other end was broken and open.

I banged on the lighthouse door and waited. "Mr. Beeston!" I called. I banged once more.

Nothing.

I looked at the key ring again, running my fingers

over its crystal edge. Oh, well. I could always give it back another time.

I buttoned the key ring into my pocket and headed home.

Chapter Eight

*T*his was it. The moment I'd been dreading. The school board had only gone and re-opened the pool! Apparently some parents made a fuss. So here we were again. I stepped through the trough of icy cold water on the way to the pool. Back at the gym, I had tried telling Mr. Bird I had a planter's wart on my foot, but he just gave me a couple of rubber socks to put on. So now the game was up, *plus* I looked ridiculous. Great. What was I going to do? Five more minutes and my secret would be revealed. Everybody would know I was a freak!

"Come on, people; we haven't got all day." Bob

clapped his hands together as I walked slowly to the side of the pool and joined the rest of the class. "It'll be time to get out again before you set foot in the water."

My heart thumped so loud I could feel it in my ears.

"Okay, those who can swim already can jump right in," he said. *Please, please don't remember that I can swim,* I prayed silently. Time was running out.

"That means you." Mandy Rushton elbowed Julia and pointed to me. "What's up, *fish girl?*" she sneered. "Have you gotten water shy all of a sudden?"

I tried to ignore her, but Bob was looking our way. "What's going on over—" Then he recognized me. "Oh, yeah. You're the one who got a cramp, aren't you?"

I stepped back toward the wall, hoping it might swallow me up and then I could disappear forever. I couldn't do it—I couldn't!

"You can get in when you're ready." *Yeah, right— no way.* "Take it easy, though. We don't want the same thing to happen again." He turned back to the others. "Come on, you guys. Let's get on with it, shall we?"

"Let's all see how the *fish girl* does it!" Mandy said loudly, and everyone turned around to look at us. Then she pushed me forward and I lost my footing. Tripping on the slippery floor, I went flying into the pool with a loud SPLASH!

For the tiniest moment, I forgot all about Mandy. She wasn't important. All that mattered was that I was in the water again, losing myself to its creamy smoothness, wrapping myself up in it as if it were my favorite dressing gown, keeping me safe and warm.

Then I remembered where I was!

I swam to the surface and looked up to see thirty pairs of eyes facing my way—at least one of them glinting nastily at me, waiting for my *freakness* to be revealed!

I had to fight it—I had to—but it was starting already! My legs were going numb, joining together. And, like an idiot, I'd swum halfway across the pool!

I heaved myself through the water, splashing and dragging my body along, keeping my legs as still as possible to try to stop my tail from forming. Bit by bit, I propelled myself to the side, my arms working like a windmill. I *had* to get there before it happened. Hurry, hurry!

Gasping and panting, I finally heaved myself out of the pool—*just* in time! The second I dragged my body over the side, my legs started to relax. Wheezing and breathless, I pulled myself out of the pool and sat on the side.

Bob was over in a second. "Have you hurt yourself?" He stared down at me, and I suddenly had an idea. I grabbed my foot.

"It's my ankle," I said. "I think I've sprained it."

Bob narrowed his eyes. "How did that happen?"

I was about to say I'd fallen in when I saw Mandy's face. Sneering and jeering at me. Why should I let her off the hook? "Mandy pushed me," I said.

"Okay, well, there'll be no swimming for either one of you this week," he said. "You can sit in the corner for the rest of the lesson," he said sternly to Mandy. Then he turned to me. "And you put that ankle up and rest it."

He clapped his hands as he went back to the class. "That's it, people, show's over. Let's do some swimming!"

It wasn't the cold that made me shiver as I limped back to the changing room. It had more to do with Mandy's words, hissed at me through clenched teeth so quietly no one else could hear.

"I'll get you back for this, fish girl," she said. "Just wait."

I hung back while Shona swam ahead, my tail flapping as we drew closer to the shipwreck. The night was crunchy with a million stars, but no moon.

"We're nearly there." Shona dove under the water. I followed her, trailing a few yards behind.

Soon, the golden light was filtering through weeds and rocks, pulling us toward the ship.

"Shona, we can't do it!" I blurted out. "There's no point."

Shona swam back to me. "But you agreed—"

"It's no good. He's not my father."

She stared at me.

"My father left us. Just like I thought he had." I told her what Mr. Beeston had said—and about his strange threat.

"Are you sure?" she asked when I'd finished.

Why would Mr. Beeston bother to lie? I'd asked myself that question so many times over the last three days. I still wasn't sure I believed him—but it was better than building up false hopes.

"I was so certain. . . ." Shona looked over her shoulder at the ship. "Look—why don't we go anyway? We're nearly there."

"What's the use?"

"What have we got to lose? And there was something I wanted to show you. Something about the door in that passageway."

What did it matter? If the ship didn't have anything to do with me, there was nothing to fear. "Okay," I said.

We slithered along the dark corridor, feeling our way back down those slimy walls. I tried hard not to make eye contact with the open-jawed fish that had followed us down.

"So what did you want to show me?" I asked as we swam.

"There was a symbol on the door. I completely forgot about it after everything that happened."

"What symbol?"

"A trident."

"What's a trident?"

"Neptune's symbol. He carries it everywhere with him. It's what he uses to create thunderstorms—or islands."

"Islands? He can create whole islands?"

"Well, that's only when he's in a good mood—so it doesn't happen much. More often he makes the biggest storms out at sea!" Shona's eyes had that wide shiny look they always did when she talked about Neptune.

"Some merfolk say he can turn you to stone with his trident. His palace is filled with stone animals. I heard that they were all animals who had disobeyed him at one time. And he can make ships disappear, just by waving it at them—or produce a feast for a hundred merpeople, or create volcanoes out of thin air."

"Cool!"

We'd arrived at the door. "Look." She pointed at the top corner of the door. A brass plate. An engraving. Quite faint—but there was no mistaking what I was looking at.

The picture from Mr. Beeston's key ring.

"But—but that's—" I pulled at my pocket. "It's impossible. It can't be!"

"What?" Shona swam up to my side. I handed her the key ring. "Where did you get this?" she asked.

"It's Mr. Beeston's."

"Sharks!" Shona breathed. "So do you think . . ." Her words trailed away into the watery darkness. What did I think? I didn't think anything anymore.

"Shall we try it?" Shona took the key from me.

I watched in amazement as it turned smoothly in the lock.

The door slid open.

Silently, we slithered inside. We were in a small office. It had a desk stacked about a yard high with laminated folders and papers held down by rocks, and a stool nailed to the floor in front of it. Shona swam to the desk and pulled on something. A second later, an orange glow burst out above me. I blinked as I got used to the sudden glare, then looked up to see where the light had come from. A long slimy creature with a piece of string on its tail clung to the ceiling.

"Electric eel," she explained.

We looked at each other in silence. "What about the other key?" she said eventually, swimming over to a metal filing cabinet in the corner. I tried the drawers, but they wouldn't pull out. I almost closed my eyes as I tried to put it in the lock at the top. *Please don't fit, please don't fit,* I said to myself. What would I find if it did?

I couldn't even get it halfway in.

I let out a huge breath and was suddenly desperate to get out of there. "Shona, maybe this is all a big mistake," I said, backing out of the office. But then I knocked my tail against the stool and slipped backward. A swarm of tiny black fish escaped from under the table, spinning out of the room and away from us.

"Emily!" Shona tugged my sleeve and pointed at something under the table.

I leaned forward to get a closer look. There was a wooden chest; quite big, with brass edging and a chain looped all around it. It was like something out of *Treasure Island*. I swam under the table, and Shona helped me drag it out. "Flipping fins," she said quietly, staring at something dangling at the front of the chain. A brass padlock.

As I slipped the key easily into the lock and the brass hook bounced from the tumbler, I wasn't even surprised. A line of silver fish pecked at the chest as I opened it. It was full of files. I grabbed a handful of them. The colors changed from blue to green as I lifted them toward me. Rummaging through the pile, I tried to pull the rest of them out. Then I came to a folder that was different from the others. For one thing, it was thicker. For another thing, it looked newer.

And for another, it had my name on it.

Chapter Nine

I don't know how long I looked at the file. I realized at some point that my hand had almost gone numb from clutching it so tightly.

"What is it?" Shona came to look over my shoulder at the files. That's when I noticed another one at the bottom of the chest. I reached down to get it. It had my mom's name on it. Below that was another. I almost didn't dare to look. I shut my eyes as I picked it up. When I opened them, I was looking at a name I'd been dreaming about for a week: Jake Windsnap.

I traced the words with my fingertips. Jake Windsnap. I said his name over and over, wondering if there was any way it could be a mistake or a practical joke or something. "Jake *is* my father," I said out loud. Of course he was. I'd known it in my heart from the first time I'd heard his name. It just took seeing it in writing to convince my brain.

I opened the file, my hands shaking so much I almost dropped all its contents. The sheets inside it were plastic. And they all had the pitchfork image at the top: Neptune's trident.

"But what in sharks' name does Mr. Beeston have to do with any of this?" Shona asked.

"Maybe he knows where my dad is, after all. I mean, if they were best friends, maybe he's trying to help him. Maybe they've been in touch all along." My words came out in a rush, none of them convincing me — or Shona, by the look on her face.

"There's only one way to find out," she said.

I held the files out in front of me. Once I'd looked inside, there would be no going back. I couldn't pretend I hadn't seen whatever was in there. Maybe I didn't want to know. I pulled at my hair, twiddling, twisting it around and around. I had to look. Whatever it said, I needed to know the truth.

I opened the file with my name on it. A scrappy bit of paper with a handwritten note scrawled across it fell on the floor. I picked it up, Shona looking over my shoulder as I read.

EW One: All clear.
Nothing to report. No mer-gene identified. Possibly negative. (50% chance.) Scale detection nil.

"What in the ocean is that supposed to mean?" asked Shona.

I shook my head, pulling a bigger sheet out of the file.

> EW Eight: Moment of truth?
> Subject has requested swimming lessons again. (See MPW file for cross-ref.) CFB present to witness request. Denied by mother. Unlikely to be granted in near future. Needs careful attention. Almost certainly negative mer-gene but experiment MUST NOT be abandoned. Continued observation—priority.

"Subject!" I spluttered. "Is that me?"

Shona winced.

Careful watch? Had he been stalking me? What if he was watching us now? I shuddered and swam over to close the office door. A lone blue fish skimmed into the room and over my head as I did.

We scanned the rest of the file. It was all the same: subjects and initials and weird stuff that didn't make sense.

I picked up my mom's file.

> MPW Zero: Objectives.
> MPW—greatest risk to merworld detection. Constant supervision by CFB. M-drug to be administered.

Shona gasped. "M-drug. I know what that is! They're wiping her memory!"

"*What?* Who is?"

"Mr. Beeston is. He must work for Neptune!"

"Work for Neptune? But how? Then he'd be a . . . I mean, he *can't*. Can he?"

Shona rubbed her lip. "They usually send people away after they've been memory wiped."

"Why?"

"It can wear off if you go near merfolk areas. We learned all about it in science last term."

"So you think they did it to my mom?"

"They probably still are. One dose is usually enough for a one-time incident—but not for a whole series of memories. They must be topping it up somehow."

Topping it up? I thought about all Mr. Beeston's visits. He wasn't lonely! He was drugging my mom!

We looked all the way through Mom's file. Page after page noting her movements. He'd been spying on us for years.

"I feel sick," I said, closing the file.

Shona picked up Jake's file. There was a note stuck on the front with something scribbled on it. East Wing: E 930. We read in silence.

JW Three: Bad influence.
JW continuing to complain about sentence. Sullen and difficult.
JW Eight: Improvement.
Subject has settled into routine of prison life. Behavior improved.
JW Eleven: Isolation.
Operation Desert Island discussed openly by prisoner. Isolation—three days.

"Operation Desert Island!" Shona exclaimed. "So it's true after all. There *is* a place! Somewhere merfolk and humans live together!"

"How do you know that's what it is?" I asked. "It could be anything."

We read on.

"None of it makes any sense," I said, swimming backward and forward across the room to help me think.

Shona continued flicking through the file. "It's all numbers and dates and weird initials." She closed the file. "I can't make fin or tail of it." She grabbed another file from the chest. "Listen to this," she said. " 'Project Lighthouse. CFB to take over Brightport Lighthouse until completion of Windsnap problem. Ground floor adapted for access. Occasional siren support available with unreliable beam. Previous lighthouse keeper: M-drug and removal from scene.' " Shona looked up.

"What are we going to do?" I whispered.

"What *can* we do? But, hey—at least you've found your dad."

My dad. The words sounded strange. Not right. Not yet. "But I *haven't* found him," I said. "That's just it. All I've found is some stupid file that doesn't make any sense."

Shona put the file down. "I'm sorry."

"Look, Shona, we know Jake's my—my father, don't we?"

"Without a doubt."

"And we know where he is?"

"Well, yes."

"And he can't come out. He's locked away. And he didn't *choose* to leave me. . . ."

"I'm *sure* he never wanted to —"

"So we'll go to him!"

Shona looked at me blankly.

I shoved the files back in the chest, locked it firmly. "Come on, let's go!"

"Go? Where?"

"The prison." I turned around to face her. "I've got to find him."

Shona's tail flapped gently. "Emily, it's *miles* away."

"We're mermaids! We can swim for miles, no problem!"

"Maybe *I* can, but it's definitely too far for you. You're only half mermaid, remember?"

"So you're saying I'm not as good as you?" I folded my arms. "I thought you were supposed to be my friend. I thought you might even have been my best friend."

Shona's tail flapped even more. "Really?" she said. "I want you to be my best friend, too."

"Well, you've got a funny way of showing it. You won't even help me find my father."

Shona winced. "I just don't think we'd make it there. I'm not even sure exactly where it *is*."

"But we'll never know if we don't try. Please, Shona. If you were *really* my best friend, you would."

"Okay," she sighed. "We'll try. But I don't want

you collapsing on me miles out at sea. If you get tired, you have to tell me, and we come back, okay?"

I shoved the chest back under the table. "Okay."

I don't know how long we'd been swimming; maybe an hour. I started to feel as if I had heavy weights attached to each arm; my tail was practically dropping off. Flying fish raced along with us, bouncing past on both sides. An occasional gull darted into the sea, like a white dart piercing the water.

"How much farther is it?" I gasped.

"We're not even halfway." Shona looked back. "Are you all right?"

"Fine." I tried not to pant while I spoke. "Great. No problem."

Shona slowed down to swim alongside me, and we carried on in silence for a bit. "You're not okay, are you?" she said after a while.

"I'm fine," I repeated, but my head slipped under the water while I spoke. I coughed as a mouthful of water went down the wrong way. Shona grabbed me.

"Thanks." I wriggled away from her. "I'm all right now."

She looked at me doubtfully. "Maybe we could both do with a rest," she said. "There's a tiny island about five minutes' swim from here. It's out of our way, but it would give us a chance to get our breath back."

"Okay," I said. "If you really need a rest, I don't mind."

"Fine." Shona swam off again. "Follow me."

Soon, we were sitting on an island barely larger than the flat rock that had become our meeting place. It was hard and gravelly, but I lay down the second I dragged myself out of the sea, the water brushing against me as my tail turned back into legs.

It seemed only seconds later that Shona gently shook my shoulder. "Emily," she whispered. "You'd better get up. It's starting to get light."

I sat up. "How long have I been asleep?"

Shona shrugged. "Not long."

"Why didn't you wake me? We'll never get there now. You did it on purpose!"

Shona squeezed her lips together and scrunched up her eyes. I thought about her pretending she needed a rest, and about taking me to her school and everything. "I'm sorry," I said. "I know why you did it."

"It's too far. It's probably even too far for me, never mind you."

"I'm *never* going to see him. I bet he doesn't even remember he's got a daughter!" I felt a drop of salty water on my cheek and wiped it roughly away. "What am I going to do?"

Shona put her arm around me. "I'm sorry," she said.

"I'm sorry, too. I shouldn't have been mean to you. You've been amazing. Really helpful."

Shona made a face at me, as if she was trying not to smile but couldn't stop a little grin from slipping out through her frown.

"And I know you're right," I added. "There's no way I could get there tonight, not if we're only halfway."

"Not even that. Look." She pointed out to the horizon. "See that big cloud that looks like a whale spurting water—with the little starfish-shaped one behind it?"

I looked up at the sky. "Um, yeah," I said uncertainly.

"Just below that, where the sea meets the sky, it's lighter than the rest of the horizon."

I studied the horizon. It looked an awfully long way away!

"That's it. The Great Mermer Reef. It's like a huge wall, bigger than anything you've ever seen in your life, made of rocks and coral in every shape and color you could imagine—and then about a hundred more. The prison's a mile beyond it. You have to go through the reef to get there."

My heart felt like a rock itself—dropping down to the bottom of the sea. "Shona, it's absolutely *miles* away."

"We'll work something out," Shona said. "I promise." Then she scrabbled around among the rocks and picked up a couple of stones. She handed one to me.

"What's this?" I looked at the stone.

"They're friendship pebbles. They mean that we're best friends — if you want to be."

"Of course I want to be!"

"See? They're almost exactly the same." She showed me her pebble. "We each keep ours on us at all times. It means we'll always be there for each other." Then she said, more quietly, "And it's also a promise that we'll find your dad."

I washed my pebble in the water; it went all shiny and smooth. "It's the best present anyone's ever given me."

Shona slipped hers into her tail and I put mine in my jacket pocket. I didn't want it to disappear when my legs returned! I looked at the patch of light that was spreading and growing across the horizon.

"Come on." Shona slid back into the sea. "We'd better get going."

We slowly made our way back to Rainbow Rocks.

"See you Sunday?" I asked as we said goodbye.

Shona's cheeks reddened a touch. "Can we make it Monday?"

"I thought you couldn't get out on Mondays."

"I will. I'll make sure of it. It's just that the Diving and Dance display is Monday morning, and I don't want to be too tired for the triple flips."

"Monday night, then." I smiled. "And good luck."

By the time I got home, I was so tired I could have fallen asleep standing up. But my head was spinning with thoughts and questions. And sadness. I'd found out where my father was, but how would we ever get there? Would we really find him? It felt like I was losing him all over again. I'd virtually lost my mom as well. If only I could make her remember!

As I tried to get to sleep, something Shona had said swam into the corner of my mind. *Sometimes it doesn't work at all, especially if you go near merfolk areas.*

Of course!

I knew *exactly* what I was going to do.

Chapter Ten

*M*om always sleeps in on Sundays. She says even God had a day of rest, and she doesn't see why she can't. I'm not allowed to disturb her until she says it's morning—which usually isn't until around noon.

I paced up and down the boat, willing her to wake up. What if she slept right through the afternoon and woke up at coffee time? Disaster! I couldn't take the risk of Mr. Beeston showing up before I'd spoken to her. So I broke a golden rule. I crept into her room and sat on the bed.

"Mom," I stage-whispered from the end of the bed. She didn't stir. I inched farther up and leaned toward her ear. "Mom," I croaked a bit louder.

She opened one eye and then closed it again. "Whadyouwan?" she grumbled.

"You have to get up."

"Whassamatter?"

"I want to go out."

Mom groaned and turned over.

"Mom, I want us to go out together."

Silence.

"Please get up."

She turned back to face me and opened her eyes a crack.

"We never do anything together," I said.

"Why now? Why can't you leave me in peace? What time is it, anyway?"

I quickly turned her alarm clock around so she couldn't see it. "It's late. Come on, Mom. *Please*."

Mom rubbed her eyes and lay on her back. "I don't suppose you're going to give me any peace until I do, are you?"

I smiled hopefully.

"Just leave me alone and I'll get up."

I didn't move. "How do I know you won't go back to sleep the minute I leave?"

"Emily! I said I'll get up and I will. Now leave me alone! And if you want to get back in my good graces, you can make me a nice cup of tea. And then I might forgive you."

Mom took a bite of her toast. "So, where do you imagine we're going, now that you've ruined my Sunday morning?"

I knew *exactly* where we were going. Shiprock Bay. The nearest you could get to Rainbow Rocks by road. I'd been studying the bus routes, and there was one that took us almost all the way there. We could get off on the coast road and walk along the head-land. It must be worth a try. I had to jog her memory somehow.

"I just thought we could have a day trip around the coast," I said casually as I popped a piece of toast and strawberry jelly in my mouth.

"What about Mr. Beeston?"

"What about him?" I nearly choked on my toast.

"We'll have to be back by three. We can't let him down."

"Oh, Mom! Can't you break your date with him for once?"

"*Emily*. Mr. Beeston is a lonely man and a good friend. How many times do I have to tell you that? You know I don't like letting him down. He has not broken our arrangement once in all these years, and I'm not about to do it to him now. And it is *not* a date!"

"Whatever." This wasn't the time to tell her what I knew about the 'lonely man.' What *did* I know, anyway? Nothing that made any sense. I swallowed hard to get my toast down. My throat was dry. We'd still have time to get there. Maybe we could accidentally-on-purpose miss the bus back. I'd think of something. I *had* to!

"This is really nice, actually." Mom looked out of the window as we bumped around the coast road. It had started to turn inland, and I was trying to figure out which stop would be best for us to try. The ocean looked completely different from this angle. Then I saw a familiar clump of rocks and decided to take a chance. I got up and rang the bell. "This is our stop," I said.

"You know, I think I'm almost glad you woke me up," Mom said as we got off the bus. "Not that that's an excuse to do it every week!" She walked over to a green bench on the headland that looked out to sea and sat down. "And you've picked such a nice spot, too."

"What are you doing?" I asked as she reached into her bag and brought out the sandwiches.

"We're having a picnic, aren't we?"

"Not *here*!"

Mom looked around. "Why not? I can't see any-where better."

"Mom, we're right by the road! Let's walk out toward the water a bit."

She frowned.

"Come on, just a little way. *Please*. You promised."

"I did no such thing!" she snapped. But she put the sandwiches back anyway, and we headed along a little headland path that led out toward the beach.

After we'd been walking for about fifteen minutes, the path came to an abrupt end. In front of us was a gravelly climb down the cliff.

"Now what?" Mom looked around.

"Let's go down there."

"You must be joking. Have you seen my shoes?"

I looked at her feet. Why hadn't I thought to tell her not to wear her platform sandals? "They're okay," I said.

"Emily. I am *not* going to break my ankles just so you can drag me off down some dangerous cliff." She turned around and started walking back.

"No, wait!" I looked around desperately. She couldn't leave — she had to see the rocks. A winding path lay almost hidden under brambles, stony and rough but not nearly as steep as the other one. "Let's try here," I said. "And look — it gets flat again over there if we can just get down this part."

"I don't know." Mom looked doubtfully down the cliff.

"Come on; let's try it. I'll go first and then I can cushion your fall if you trip and go flying." I tried an impish smile, and she gave in.

"If I break my legs, you're bringing me breakfast in bed every day until I'm better."

"Deal."

I picked my way through the brambles and stones, checking behind me every few seconds to make sure Mom was still there. We managed to get down to the rocks in one piece.

Mom rubbed her elbow. "Ouch. Thorns." She pulled up a piece of seaweed and rubbed it on her arm. I gazed in front of us. Just a few yards of water separated us from Rainbow Rocks. I couldn't help smiling as I watched the sea washing over the flat rocks, rainbow water caressing them with every wave.

"Mom?"

"Hmm?"

I took a deep breath. "Do you believe in mermaids?" I asked, my throat tight and strained.

Mom laughed. "Mermaids? Oh, Emily, you do ask some silly—"

But then she stopped. She dropped the seaweed on the ground. Looking out to sea, her face went all hard.

"What is it, Mom?" I asked gently.

"Where are we?" she whispered.

"Just by the coast. I just thought it'd be nice to go out for—"

"What is this place?"

I hadn't actually thought about what I'd say once we got here! What would she do if she knew—not just about Jake but about me, too? What if she only half remembered? She might think we were *both* freaks. Maybe she'd be ashamed of us. Why hadn't I thought this through?

I cleared my throat. "Um, it's just some rocks," I said carefully. "Isn't it?"

Mom turned to me. "I've been here before," she said, her face scrunched up as if she was in pain.

"When?"

"I don't know. But I know this place."

"Shall we go farther down?"

"No!" She turned back the way we'd come. "Emily. We have to go back. Mr. Beeston will be expecting us."

"But we just got here. Mr. Beeston won't be around for ages yet."

"I can't stay here," Mom said. "I've got a bad feeling about it. We're going home." She started walking back so quickly I could hardly keep up.

We ate our sandwiches on that green bench on the headland, after all. A bus went whizzing past just as we were approaching the road, so there was nothing to do but wait for the next one. We ate in silence: me not knowing what to say, Mom gazing into space.

I kept wanting to ask her things, or tell her things, but where could I start?

Eventually another bus came, and we rode home in

silence as well. By the time we got back to Brightport Pier, it was nearly four o'clock.

"Are you angry with me?" I asked as we let ourselves into the boat.

"Angry? Why? You haven't done anything wrong, have you?" Mom searched my face.

"I wanted to have a nice day out and now you've gotten all sad."

Mom shook her head. "Just thoughtful, sweetheart. There was something about that place. . . ." Her voice trailed off.

"What? What was it?"

"It was such a strong memory, but I don't even know what it was." She shook her head again and took her coat off. "Listen to me, talking drivel as usual."

"You're not talking drivel at all," I said urgently. "What was the memory?"

Mom hugged her coat. "Do you know, it wasn't a memory of a *thing*. More a feeling of something. I felt an overwhelming feeling of . . . love."

"Love?"

"And then something else. Sadness. Enormous sadness." Mom took her coat down to the engine room to hang it up. "I told you I was talking nonsense, didn't I?" she called. "Now get that teakettle on, and I'll go and give Mr. Beeston a shout. I'll bet he's wondering where we've been."

I glanced out of the window as I filled the kettle. Mr. Beeston was on his way up the pier! My whole body shivered. He was striding fast and didn't look happy.

POUND! POUND! POUND! He banged on the roof as Mom came back in the kitchen.

"Oh, good. He's here." Mom went to let him in. "Hello." She smiled. "I was just coming to—"

"Where have you been?" he demanded.

"We've been out for a little adventure, haven't we Emily? Just up along the—"

"I was here at three o'clock," he snapped, stabbing a finger at his watch. "I waited a whole hour. What's the meaning of this?" His head snapped across to face me. I swallowed hard.

Mom frowned at us both. "Come on, there's no need to get upset," she said. "Let's have some coffee." She went to get the cups and saucers. "What have you got for us today, Mr. B.? Some lovely cinnamon buns? With vanilla glaze?"

"Doughnuts," Mr. Beeston said without taking his eyes off me.

"I haven't done anything," I said.

"Of course you haven't, Emily. Who said you did? Now, won't you please join us?" Mom held a cup out to Mr. Beeston as he finally turned away. He took his jacket off and folded it over the back of a chair.

"No, thanks." I lay on the sofa and eavesdropped, waiting for Mr. Beeston to try to inject her with the memory drug. I had to catch him in the act, to prove to Mom that he wasn't really her friend. But what if he got to me first? What if he injected *me* with the memory drug, too?

But he didn't do anything. As soon as he sat down with Mom, he acted as though nothing had happened. They just drank their coffee and munched doughnuts and chatted about condo owners and the price of mini golf.

They'd barely finished eating when Mr. Beeston glanced at his watch. "Well, I've got to move along," he said.

"You're going?" But he hadn't drugged her yet! Maybe he didn't do it every week. Well, I'd be waiting for him as soon as he tried!

"I have a four-forty-five appointment," he growled, the left side of his mouth twitching as he spoke. "And *I* don't like to keep people waiting."

I didn't say anything.

"Goodbye, Mary P." He let himself out.

Mom started clearing the cups away, and I grabbed a hand towel.

"So you were saying earlier," I began as Mom handed me a saucer to dry.

"Saying?"

"About our outing."

"Oh, of course—the little trip to the headland," Mom smiled. "Lovely, wasn't it?"

"Not just the headland," I said. "The rocks."

Mom looked at me blankly.

"Rainbow Rocks . . ." The words caught in my throat as I held my breath.

"Rainbow what?"

"Mom—don't tell me you've forgotten! The rocks, the rainbow colors when the sea washed over them, the way you felt when we were there. Love. And sadness and stuff?"

Mom laughed. "You know, Mrs. Partington told me at our last parent-teacher conference that you had a good imagination. Now I know what she means."

I stared at her as she bustled around the galley, straightening the tablecloth and brushing crumbs off chairs with her hands.

"What?" She looked up.

"Mom, what do you think we were talking about before Mr. Beeston came around?"

Mom shut one eye and rubbed her chin. "Heck— give me a minute." She looked worried for a moment, then laughed. "You know—I can't remember. Gone! Never mind. Now bring me the broom and dustpan. We can't leave the carpet like this."

I continued to stare at her. She'd forgotten! He *had* drugged her, after all! But how? And when?

"Come on, shake a leg. Or do I have to get them myself?"

I fetched the broom and pan out of the cupboard and handed them to her.

"Mom . . ." I tried again as she swept under the table. "Do you *really* not remem—"

"Emily." Mom sat up on her knees and spoke firmly. "A joke is a joke, and any joke is usually not funny after a while. Now, I don't want to hear any more nonsense

about multicolored rocks, if you don't mind. I've got more important things to do than play along with your daydreams."

"But it's not a—"

"EMILY."

I knew that tone of voice. It meant it was time to shut up. I picked up the doughnut bags from the table and went to throw them away. Then I noticed some writing on one of the bags: *MPW*.

"Why does this one have your initials on it?" I asked.

"I don't know. Probably so he knows which doughnuts are mine."

"What difference does it make?"

"Come on, Emily, everbody knows I've got a sweet tooth. I always get the ones with more sugar."

"But can't you tell which ones have more sugar just by looking at them?"

"Emily, why are you being so difficult today? And what do you have against Mr. Beeston? I *won't* have you talking about him like this. I'm not listening to another word."

"But I don't understand! Why can't he just look in the bag?"

Mom ignored me. Then she started whistling and I gave up and went back to my cabin. I took the bags with me. They held some kind of answer, I was sure of it—if only I could figure out what it was.

I stared so hard at her initials that my eyes started to water.

And then, as the letters blurred under my gaze, it hit me so hard that I nearly fell over. Of course! The memory drug!

He gave it to her in the doughnuts.

Chapter Eleven

When I got home from school on Monday, I slumped on the sofa and threw my backpack on the floor. Mom was reading. "Did you have a nice day?" she asked, folding over the corner of the page and putting her book down.

"Mm." I got a glass of milk out of the fridge.

I could hardly stand to look at her. How was I ever going to make her believe me? Somehow I had to make her see for herself what Mr. Beeston was up to. *Plus* I still had to find my father.

A gentle rap on the roof startled me out of my thoughts. I clenched my fists. If that was Mr. Beeston, I'd—

"Hello, Emily," Millie said in a mysterious kind of way as she unwrapped herself from her large black cloak.

"Are you going out tonight?" I asked Mom.

"It's the Bay Residents' Council meeting. I told you last week."

"You did?"

"Nice to see I'm not the only one around here with the memory of a goldfish." She tweaked my cheek as she passed me.

I checked my watch. "But it's only six o'clock!"

"I need to get there early to open up. It's at the bookshop," she called from down the corridor. "Thanks for this, Millie," she added as she came back in with her coat. "Get out the sofa bed if I'm late."

"I might just do that," Millie replied. "My energy is a little depleted today. I think it's the new ginkgo biloba tablets on top of my shiatsu."

"Sounds likely," Mom said, doing up her coat. Another knock on the roof made me jump again.

"Heavens to Betsy, Emily, you're a bit twitchy tonight, aren't you?" Mom ruffled my hair as Mr. Beeston's face appeared at the door.

I froze.

"Only me," he said, scanning the room without coming in.

"You didn't tell me *he* was going," I whispered, grabbing at her coat while Mr. Beeston waited outside.

"Of course he's going—he's the chairman!" she whispered back. "And he's offered to help me set up," she added. "Which is nice of him, by the way."

"Mom, I don't want you to go!"

"Don't want me to go? What on earth are you talking about?"

What could I say? How could I get her to believe me? She wouldn't hear a word against Mr. Beeston — the sweet, kind, lonely man. Well, I'd prove to her that he wasn't anything of the kind!

"I just —"

"Come on, now. Don't be a baby." She pried my fingers from her sleeve. "Millie's here to look after you. I'm just up at the shore if you need me urgently. And I mean *urgently*." She gave me a quick peck, rubbed my cheek with her thumb — and was gone.

"How come you don't go to the Bay Residents' meetings, Millie?"

"Oh, I don't believe in all that democratic fuss and nonsense," she said, shifting me up the sofa so she could sit down.

We sat silently in front of the television. Once her first show had finished, I waited for her to tell me it was bedtime. But she didn't. I looked across at the sofa; she lay on her side, her eyes closed, mouth slightly open.

"Millie?" I whispered. No reply. She was fast asleep! When would I get an opportunity like this again? I had to do it.

The Great Mermer Reef might be too far to swim —but it wouldn't be too far by boat! And now was the perfect time. In fact, it might be my only chance.

Could I do it? *Really?* I looked at the clock. Half past eight. Mom wouldn't be back for ages yet, and Millie was fast asleep.

I grabbed the engine key from the peg and crept outside. There was probably another half an hour or so before it was dark. I could handle the darkness now anyway; I'd gotten used to the sea at night.

But would I remember how to operate the boat? I'd only done it a few times. We have to go around to Southpool Harbor every couple of years to get the hull checked out, and Mom usually lets me take it some of the way. We hardly ever use the sail. I don't know why we have it, really.

The pier was quiet except for all the masts clinking and chattering in the wind. I pulled at my hair, twisting it frantically around my fingers. I probably looked like somebody about to take their first bungee jump. But I simply had to do it, however dangerous or scary or insane it might be.

Uncoiling the ropes, I had one last look down the pier. Deserted . . .

Almost.

Someone was coming out of the arcade. I ducked below the mast and waited. It was Mandy's mom! She was heading down the pier, probably to the meeting. And a figure was standing in the doorway of the arcade. Mandy!

I ducked down again, waited for her to go back inside. Had she seen me?

The rope slackened in my hands — I was drifting away from the jetty. Close enough to jump back and pull the boat in again — but floating farther away by the second. *What should I do?* There was still time to abandon the whole thing.

Then a breeze lifted the front of the boat off the water and, without any more thinking on my part, the decision was made. I glanced back. She'd gone. I hurled the rope onto the jetty and turned the ignition key.

Nothing happened.

I tried again. It started this time, and I held my breath as its familiar *dunka dunka dunka* broke into the silence of the evening.

"HEY!"

I turned around.

"Fish girl!"

It was Mandy! She stepped onto our dock.

"What d'you think you're doing?" she called.

"Nothing!" *Nothing?* What kind of a stupid thing was that to say?

"Oh, I know. Are you running away now that Julia doesn't want to be your friend?"

"What?"

"She doesn't want to know you anymore, after you blew her off last weekend. Lucky she had me there to make her see *someone* cares about her feelings." Mandy paused as she let an evil smile crawl across her face.

"Your mom knows you're taking the boat out, I assume?"

"Of course!" I said quickly. "I'm just moving it over to Southpool."

"Yeah. Shall we check?" She waved her cell phone in front of her.

"You wouldn't!"

"No? Want to make a bet? You think I haven't been *waiting* for an opportunity like this? Little miss goody-goody two shoes, making out like you're soooo sweet and innocent."

The boat bobbed farther away from the dock. "Why do you hate me so much?" I called over the engine.

"Hmm. Let me think." She put her finger dramatically to her mouth and looked away, as though talking to an audience. "She gets me grounded, steals my best friend, turns the swimming teacher against me. She's a great big fat SHOWOFF!" Mandy looked back at me. "I really don't know."

Then she turned and started walking back up the jetty, waving her phone in the air.

"Mandy, don't! Please!"

"Maybe I will, maybe I won't," she called over her shoulder. "See ya."

What should I do? I couldn't go back. I *couldn't*. This was probably my one and only chance to find my father. And Mandy Rushton was NOT going to ruin it. I forced her words out of my mind. She wasn't going to stop me—she *wasn't*!

I turned my attention back to my plan.

Minutes later, I was edging away from the pier, holding the tiller and carefully navigating my way out of the harbor. I went over what I'd done when I'd driven the boat to Southpool—and tried hard to convince myself that what I was doing now really wasn't very different.

As I sailed out to sea, I looked back at Brightport Bay. The last rays of the sun winked and glinted on the water like tiny spotlights. Ocean spray dusted my hair.

I closed my eyes for a second while I thought about what I was doing. I had to find the Great Mermer Reef. Based on the time Shona and I had gotten halfway there, I knew more or less where it was, so I studied the horizon and aimed for the section that was lighter than the rest. The part that would shimmer a hundred colors when I got close by.

It got dark very suddenly as we sliced slowly through the water. *King* never does anything in a hurry. My hand was getting cold, holding on to the tiller. And I was getting wet. *King* bounced on the water, gliding along with the swells, then rising and bumping down over the waves. It had been quite calm when I set off. The farther out I got, the more hilly the sea became.

Above me, stars appeared, one by one. Soon, the night sky was packed. A fat half-moon sat among them, its other half a silhouette, semivisible as though impatient for its turn to come.

King swayed from side to side, lumbering slowly through the peaks and troughs. Was I getting anywhere? I looked behind me. Brightport was miles away! If I closed one eye and held up my hand, I could hide the whole town behind my thumbnail.

Up and down we went, climbing the waves, bouncing on the swells, inching ever closer to the Great Mermer Reef.

My eyes watered as I strained to keep them on the patch of light on the horizon, shimmering and glowing and coming gradually closer. I let myself dream about Jake — about my dad.

I'd get into the prison and we'd escape. Hiding him in the boat, we'd cruise back to the pier before anyone even realized he was gone. Then Mom would come home from the meeting. Dad would be waiting in the sea at the end of the pier, and I'd ask Mom to come for a walk with me. Then I'd leave her there on her own for a minute, and he would appear. They'd see each other, and it would be like they'd never been apart. Mom would remember everything, and we'd all live happily ever after. *Excellent* plan.

Excellent daydream, anyhow. A "plan" was something I didn't exactly have.

"EMILY!" A voice shattered my thoughts. I spun around, searching the night sky. There was a shape behind me — a long way away but coming nearer. A boat, one of those little motorboats with outboard engines that they hire out in the summer. As it got closer, I could see an outline of two people, one leaning forward in the front, one in the back at the tiller.

"Emily!" A woman's voice. And not just any woman. Mom!

Then I recognized the other voice.

"Come back here, young lady! Whatever you think you are doing, you had better stop it—and *now!*"

Mr. Beeston!

I shoved the tiller across and quickly swapped sides as the boat changed direction, pushing the throttle as far forward as it would go. *Come on, come on,* I prayed. The boat sputtered and chugged in reply but didn't speed up.

"What are you doing here?" I shouted over the engine and the waves.

"What am *I* doing here?" Mom called back. "Emily, what are YOU doing?"

"But your meeting!"

The motorboat edged closer. "The meeting got cancelled when Mrs. Rushton's girl phoned in a state. She thought you might be in danger."

I should have known she'd do it! I don't know how I could have thought even for a moment that she wouldn't.

"I'm sorry, Mom," I called. "I've got to do this. You'll understand, honestly. Trust me."

"Oh, please come back, darling," Mom called. "Whatever it is, we can sort it out."

King's engine sputtered again and seemed to be slowing down. Seawater soaked my face as we bounced on the waves, rolling and peaking like a mountain range.

"Look what you're doing to your mother," Mr. Beeston shouted. "I won't have it, do you hear me? I won't allow it."

I ran my sleeve over my wet face. "You can't tell me what to do," I shouted back, anger pushing away my fear—and any desire to keep my stupid promise to Mr. Beeston. "It's not like you're my father or anything."

Mr. Beeston didn't reply. He was concentrating hard and had almost caught up with me. Meanwhile, the shimmering light on the horizon was glowing and growing bigger all the time. I could almost see the different colors. *Come on, King,* I said under my breath. *It's not much farther now.* I looked back at the motorboat. Mom was covering her face with her hands. Mr. Beeston held the tiller tight, his face all pinched and contorted.

"You remember my father?" I called to him. "You know, your 'best friend.' What kind of a person lies to their best friend's wife for years? *Huh?*"

"I don't know what foolish ideas you've gotten into your head, child, but you had better put an end to them right now. Before I put an end to them for you." Mr. Beeston's eyes shone like a cat's as he caught mine. "Can't you see how much you are upsetting your mother?"

"Upsetting my mother? Ha! Like *you* care!"

"Emily, *please*," Mom called, her arms stretched out toward me. "Whatever it is, we'll talk about it. Don't blame Mr. Beeston. He's only trying to help."

"Come *on, King*!" I said out loud as the engine crackled and popped. "Mom." I turned to face her. They were only a couple of yards away from me now. "Mr. Beeston isn't who he says he is. And he's *not* trying to help you."

Then the engine died.

"What's the *matter* with this thing?" I shouted.

"You know we never keep much diesel onboard," Mom called. "It's a fire hazard."

"What? Who told you that?" I was in despair.

"I did," Mr. Beeston called. "Don't want you injuring yourselves, do I?" He smiled his creepy smile at me.

That was it. I stood up and lurched forward to grab the mast. I'd have to sail the rest of the way!

I uncleated the mainsheet to free the boom — that's the wooden pole that runs along the bottom of the sail. Then I undid the main halyard (the rope at the base of the mast) and hoisted the mainsail.

As a gust of wind filled the sail, the boom swung out wildly over the water. I grabbed for the mainsheet — that's the rope that controls the boom — but the gust sent its whole length running right out of the cleat and out of reach. I watched helplessly as my last hope unraveled with it.

"Oh, Emily, please stop it," Mom shouted as the boat lurched to the side. "You don't need to upset yourself like this. I know what it's about."

"*What?* If you know, what are you doing in there with him?"

"It's natural for you to feel like this, darling. Mr. Beeston told me about you being a little jealous, and how that might make you try to turn me against him. But he's just a friend. There's no need for you to go fretting like this."

The shimmering was really close now. I could see colors and lights dancing on the surface of the water. It was like a fireworks display. I groaned. "Mom, it's not—"

I broke off when I saw Mom's stricken face. It looked like those performance artists on the board-walk who pretend to be statues. In a soft voice that I barely recognized, she said, "No one could ever take the place of your father." She was gazing wide-eyed at the lights on the water.

"*My father?*"

For a moment, everything stood completely still, like a photo. The sea stopped moving; Mr. Beeston let go of the tiller; my mom and I locked eyes as though seeing each other for the first time.

Then Mr. Beeston leaped into action. "That's it," he yelled. "I'm coming aboard."

"Wait!" I shouted as a wave caught the side of the

boat. *King* lurched sideways, the sail swinging across to the other side.

Mr. Beeston had just pulled himself aboard when — *thwack!* — the boom swung back again and knocked him flying.

"Aaarrrgghh!" He clutched his head as he fell backward. Crashing to the deck with a thump, he lay flat on his back without moving.

Mom screamed and stood up. The motorboat rocked wildly.

"Mom — be careful!" I ran to the side and leaned over. "Get on," I shouted. She was alongside *King*.

Mom didn't move.

"You have to get onboard. Come on, Mom." I held an arm out. "I'll help you."

"I — I can't," she said woodenly.

"You can, Mom. You've *got* to." I scrabbled around in the bench seat and pulled out a life jacket. *King* rocked like the coin-operated bucking bronco at the arcade. The sail was still waving off to the side, the mainsheet dangling hopelessly out of reach. Holding tight to the railing, I threw the life jacket to Mom. "You'll be fine," I called. "Just get onboard fast before you drift away."

She stared at me.

"Do it!"

Mom stood up in her rocky boat, the life jacket on, and suddenly lunged for the steps. I grabbed her hand as she pulled herself onto the deck.

"Oh, Emily," she said. "I'm so sorry."

"What for?"

"It's all my fault," Mom said, holding on to me with one hand and the railing with the other as we swayed from side to side.

"Of course it's not your fault, Mom. If it's anyone's fault, it's Mr. Beeston's. He's not what he seems, Mom; he's been—"

Mom put her finger over my lips. "I know why we're here."

"You—you—"

"I remember." Mom pulled me toward her and held me tight. Over her shoulder, I could see the water shimmering and sparkling like an electric light show. The Great Mermer Reef.

I wriggled out of Mom's grasp. "You remember—what?"

Mom hesitated. "It's all a bit hazy," she said.

All at once, the sky exploded with light. "Look!" I pointed behind her. Pink lights danced below the water while a dozen colors jumped in the air above it.

"I know this place," Mom said, her voice shaking. "He—he brought me here."

"Who? Mr. Beeston?" I glanced nervously across at him. He still hadn't moved. Mom clutched the railing as the boat tilted again, and I made my way over to join her. Her face seemed to be covered in spray from the sea, but when I looked more closely, I realized it wasn't seawater at all. It was tears. "On our first anniversary," she said.

She'd been here with my dad?

"He told me this was where they would take him when they caught him."

"*Who* would take him?"

"If they ever found out about us. He knew they'd get him in the end. We both knew it, but we couldn't stop. Because we loved each other so much."

Mom's body sagged; I put my arms around her.

"I'm going to find him," I said, holding her tighter. "That's why I took the boat. I did it for all of us."

"I can't bear it," she said. "I can remember everything now. How could I have forgotten him? He was taken away because he loved me, and I forgot all about him. How can I ever forgive myself?"

"Mom, it's not your fault! You didn't just *forget* him."

"I did," she gulped. "You know I did. You asked about him and I didn't even know. I couldn't remember anything."

"But you weren't to blame."

Mom wiped a curtain of wet hair off her face and looked at me. "Who was, then?"

I nodded a thumb behind me. "Mr. Beeston," I whispered.

"Oh, Emily. Don't start with that claptrap again!"

"It's NOT claptrap!" I tried to keep my voice down. I didn't want him to wake up and ruin everything. "It's true," I whispered. "He's not what he seems."

"Emily, please don't make this worse than it is."

"Mom, *listen* to me," I snapped.

She caught my eyes for just a second, but then

looked at Mr. Beeston. "We should see how he is."
Mom shook herself free from my grasp and stumbled
along the deck to him.

"He'll be fine," I said. "Don't worry about him."

Mom ignored me and crouched down next to
him. I crouched down beside her as she leaned over
his chest and listened. Then she looked up at me, her
face paler than the million stars shining above us.

"Oh, my God," she said. "I think we've killed him."

Chapter Twelve

There's no heartbeat," Mom said, rocking back on her heels.

I opened my mouth. What could I say? A second later, the side door suddenly swung open with a bang. Mom and I grabbed each other's arms.

Millie's face appeared in the doorway.

"Do you think there's anything either of you would like to share with me?" she asked as she hitched up her long skirt and clambered out onto the deck.

Mom and I looked at each other.

"I'm sensing some . . . disorientation."

"No time now," Mom said, beckoning Millie over. "We have to do something. Mr. Beeston has had an accident. I think he's dead." She clapped a fist to her mouth.

Millie struggled over to join us, slipping and swaying on the wet deck. "Let's have a look," she said, kneeling down beside Mr. Beeston. She undid his coat and lifted up his sweater. He was wearing a thick, padded jacket of some sort underneath. I flinched as I noticed a picture of Neptune's trident sewn onto a pocket.

"Armored vest?" Millie murmured. "Now why in the blinking cosmos would he need something like that?"

I didn't say anything.

"Well, that's your answer, anyway, Mary P." Millie turned to Mom. "You wouldn't hear a ten-ton truck through that."

Just then, the boat jolted to the side. I slid across the deck and bumped against the bench seat.

"Emily, get the tiller!" Millie ordered, suddenly in charge.

I did what she said, not that it made much difference. The boat dipped and swayed helplessly in the waves.

Millie reached under Mr. Beeston's back and unbuckled the vest. Lifting it off, she bent over him, her ear to his chest. Mom came over and grabbed my hand while we waited.

"Absolutely fine," Millie announced a few seconds later.

"Oh, thank heavens." Mom hugged me. "I'd never have forgiven myself if anything had happ—"

"He just needs his chakras realigned," Millie continued. "A bit of reflexology should do it."

She pulled off Mr. Beeston's shoes and socks and settled herself at his feet. Placing her hands across her large chest, she closed her eyes and breathed in deeply. Then she lifted his right foot and started to massage it. A moment later, his foot twitched. She carried on massaging. He twitched again, this time his leg jerking about in the air. The twitching and jerking spread up his body until it reached his face and he started giggling. He was soon laughing loudly. Eventually, he leaped up, screaming, "Stop, stop!"

Millie released his foot and stood up. "Never fails," she said, wiping her hands on her skirt and heading back inside. "Give me a minute or two. Reflexology always drains my chi."

Mom went over to Mr. Beeston. "Thank heavens you're all right."

Mr. Beeston straightened his coat as he glanced at me. "Just a scratch," he said. "No harm done." A red path was worming its way down the side of his head.

My hand tightened on the tiller. "No harm done? Do you *think*?"

"Emily, this is no time to start your nonsense again.

144

What on earth have you got against the poor man?"

"What have I got against the poor man? Where do you want me to start?" I looked him in the eyes. "Is it the fact that he's been wiping your memory since the day I was born, or the fact that he's been spying on us *forever*?"

Mom didn't speak for a second. Then she laughed. "Oh, Emily, I've never heard such—"

"It's true." Mr. Beeston spoke, his eyes still locked onto mine. "She's right."

"What?" Mom held tightly on to the mast with one hand; with the other, she clutched her chest.

"It's too late, Mary P. I can't pretend anymore. And I won't. Why should I?"

"What are you talking about?" Mom looked from Mr. Beeston to me. I didn't say anything. Let him explain it.

Mr. Beeston sat down on the bench opposite me. "It was for your own good," he said. "All of you." His hands were still clutching his head, his hair all mangled and tangled up with blood and sweat and seawater.

"What was for my own good?" Mom's face hardened and grew thinner as she spoke.

"The two worlds—they don't belong together. It doesn't work." He leaned forward, his head almost between his knees. "And I should know," he added, his voice almost a whisper. "You're not the only one to grow up without a father." He spoke to the floor. "Mine disappeared the minute I was born, he did.

Just like all the others. Fishermen. All very nice having an unusual girlfriend, isn't it? Taming a beautiful siren. Show off to your friends about that, can't you?"

A tear fell from his face onto the deck. He brushed his cheek roughly. "But it's a bit different when your own son sprouts a tail! Don't want to know then, do you?"

"What are you saying?" Mom's voice was as tight as her face, her hand still gripping the mast. The sea lifted us up and down; the sail still flapped uselessly over the water.

"You can't put humans and merfolk together and expect it to work. It doesn't. All you get is pain." Finally, Mr. Beeston raised his head to look at us. "I was trying to save you from that. From what I've been through myself."

The boat shook violently as another wave hit us. I clutched the tiller more tightly. "I told you he wasn't really your friend," I hissed to Mom, the wind biting my face.

"Friendship?" he spat. "Loyalty is all that matters. To Neptune and the protection of the species. That is my life." He held up a fist across his chest. Then he glanced at Mom. His fist fell open. "That's to say," he faltered, "I mean — look, I never wanted to . . ." His voice trailed away, his chin dropping to his chest.

Mom looked like she'd been hit over the head herself. Her face was as white as the sail and her body had gone rigid. "I often wondered why they got a new lighthouse keeper so suddenly," she said. "No one ever did quite explain what happened to old Bernard. You just appeared one day. And something else I've never really thought about—you never invited me in. Not once in twelve years. Not like Bernard. We used to go up there all the time when I was younger, up on the top deck, looking all around with binoculars and telescopes. But you—my *friend*—you always kept the door closed to me. And to think I actually felt sorry for you."

The boat was starting to careen up and down, the sea getting wilder as we held the tiller together. She put her hand on my arm. "He saw you once," she said quietly to me in the darkness. "At Rainbow Rocks. Held you against his chest at the water's edge. I wouldn't let him take you in the water. Maybe if he had . . ." Her words slipped away as she looked at me, her hair plastered across her face with seawater. "I've lost twelve years."

I bit my lip, tasting salty water.

"Hidden from my own mind like everything else." She stood up and inched over toward Mr. Beeston. "You stole my life from me," she said, anger creeping into her voice. "You're nothing but a thief! A nasty, rotten, scheming THIEF!"

"Hey now, hold on a minute!" Mr. Beeston stood up. "I've been *good* to you. I've looked *after* you. You should hear what some of them wanted to —"

"You had no right." Mom shook his arm, tears rolling down her cheeks. "He is my husband. Who do you think you are?"

"Who do I think I am? I know *exactly* who I am! I'm Charles—" He stopped. Glanced briefly at Mom and took a breath. Then he suddenly thrust out his chin, his eyes clear and focused for a brief moment. "I am Charles Finright Beeston, adviser to Neptune, and I have conducted my duties with pride and loyalty for twelve years."

"How dare you!" Mom snapped. "All these years, pretending to be my friend."

"Now, wait a minute. I wasn't—I mean, I *am* your friend. You think I didn't care about you? It's for your own good. We had to put a stop to it. It's wrong, unnatural—dangerous, even—don't you see?"

Mom paused for a moment, then flew at him, bashing her fists against his chest. "All I can see is a beast. A despicable worm!" she screamed.

Mr. Beeston backed away from her. As she went for him, Mom tripped and nearly fell flat on her face. She stopped herself by clutching a rope tied onto the mast. The rope ripped loose in her hand, tearing the canvas that held the boom in place. All three of us watched as the boom drifted away from us and the sail flapped over the water even more uselessly than before.

We'd never get *anywhere* now.

I tried to hold the tiller steady as the boat lurched again. The waves were getting choppier, throwing us all over the deck. "We need to do something," I said, my voice quivering.

"I'll fix it," Mr. Beeston said, his words slow and deliberate, his eyes cold and determined. Then he turned and walked along the side of the boat to the door, holding the railing as the boat rocked.

"Mom, what are we going to do?" I asked as the waves rolled us from side to side again. Mom's steely eyes followed Mr. Beeston down the boat.

"Forget him," I said. "We need to think of something or we'll never get home again — never mind seeing Jake."

"Oh, Emily, do you really think we're going to find —"

"I know where he is," I said. "We can do it. We're nearly there!"

Mom pulled her eyes away from Mr. Beeston. "Okay. Come on," she said, snapping into action. She lifted the lid up off the bench, rummaged through hose pipes and foot pumps. "Put this on." She passed me a life jacket that was much too small for me.

"Mom. I don't need one."

"Just to be on the safe —" She stopped and looked at my legs. "Oh, golly," she said. "You mean you can . . . you're a —"

"Didn't you know?" I asked. "Didn't you ever suspect?"

She shook her head sadly. "How could I have? Maybe somewhere in the back of my mind, but I . . ."

A massive wave crashed over the side, washing away the rest of her sentence and drenching us both.

"Mom, I'm scared," I yelped, wiping the spray off my face. "It's too far even for me to swim back from here. We'll never make it."

As I spoke, the boat gave one more enormous lurch to the side. I fell to the floor, slipped across the deck. As I clutched the railing and tried to pull myself up again, I noticed a shape in the sea in front of us. A fin! That was it, then. The boat was going to capsize; we'd be eaten by sharks!

Mom has never been religious, and she's always said it's up to me to make my mind up when I was ready. I never was before. Until then.

Without even wondering what to say, I put my hands together, closed my eyes, and prayed.

Chapter Thirteen

*M*y lips moved soundlessly behind my hands, scanning all the words I could summon up: half-remembered prayers from half-listened-to visits to friends' churches. *Why didn't I pay more attention?* I asked myself. When I got to, 'Thy will be done on earth as it is in heaven,' I couldn't for the life of me think what came next.

"*Emily!*" Mom was tugging at my arm.

I shook her off. "I'm busy."

Mom tugged again. "I think you should take a look."

I opened my fingers wide enough to sneak a peek between them. It was hard to see anything, actually;

the boat was careening up and down so much. I felt even more giddy and reached out for the railing. That was when I heard it—someone calling my name! I looked at Mom even though I knew it hadn't been her. Holding the railing beside me, she pointed out to the mountainous waves with her free hand.

"Emily!" a familiar voice called again. Then a familiar head poked out above the waves, bobbing up and down in the swell. It was Shona! She grinned and waved at me.

"What are you doing here?" I shouted.

"It's Monday. You didn't show up at the rocks. I've been looking for you."

"Oh, Shona, I'm so sorry."

"When you didn't come, I had a funny feeling you'd be doing something like this!"

"I've messed it all up," I called, my throat clogged up. "We're never going to get there now."

"Don't be too sure!" she called back. "Throw me a rope. I'll see if I can tow you."

"But the boat must weigh a ton!"

"Not in water it doesn't, so long as I can get some momentum going with my tail. We do it in P.E. all the time."

"Are you sure?"

"Let's just give it a try, okay?"

"Okay," I said uncertainly, and with a flick of her tail, she was gone. Shona's tail! Of course! Not a shark fin at all!

I made my way up to the front deck, untied a rope and threw it down. Mom came with me. I tried to avoid looking at her, but I could feel her eyes boring into the side of my face. "What?" I asked without turning to her.

"Is she a . . . friend of yours?" Mom asked carefully.

"Mmm-hmm."

Mom sighed. "We've got a lot of catching up to do, don't we, sweetie?"

I carried on looking ahead. "Do you think I'm a freak?"

"A freak?" Mom reached over to pick up one of my hands. "Darling, I couldn't be more proud."

Still holding my hand, she put her other arm around me. The boat had leveled out again, and I snuggled into Mom's shoulder; wet, cold, and frightened. Neither of us spoke for a few minutes while we watched Shona pull us ever nearer to the prison—and Jake.

A few moments later, Mom and I caught each other's eyes, the same thought coming into our minds. *Where is Mr. Beeston?*

"He might be hiding," Mom said.

"I think we should check it out."

Mom stood up. "I'll go."

"I'm coming with you."

She didn't argue as we stood up and edged our way down the side of the boat. The deck was still soaking, and it was a slippery trip to the door.

I pushed my head inside. Mr. Beeston was standing

by a window in the saloon, his back to us, the window pushed open and a large shell in his hands.

"A conch? What on earth is he doing with that?" Mom whispered.

Mr. Beeston put the shell to his mouth.

"Talking to it?" I whispered back.

He muttered quietly into the shell.

"What's he saying?" I looked at Mom.

She shook her head. "Stay here," she ordered. "Crouch down behind the door. Don't let him see you. I'll be back in a second."

"Where are you going?" But she'd slid back outside. I hunched low and waited for her to return.

Two minutes later, Mom was back with a huge fishing net in her arms. "What are you doing with—"

Mom shushed me with a finger over her lips and crept inside. She beckoned me to follow.

Mr. Beeston was still leaning out of the window, talking softly into his conch. Mom inched toward him, and I tiptoed behind her. When we were right behind him, she passed me one end of the net and mouthed, "Three . . . two . . ."

When she mouthed, "One," I threw my side of the net over Mr. Beeston's head. Mom did the same on her side.

"What the—" Mr. Beeston dropped the conch and fell back into a chair.

"Quick, wrap it around him," Mom urged.

I ran in a circle around him, dragging the net with

me. Mr. Beeston struggled and lashed out, but we kept wrapping, like when someone's dog runs up to you in the park and knots your ankles together with its leash. Only better.

Mom pushed him back into his chair and lifted his legs up. "Get his feet," she demanded, dodging his kicks. I slipped under his legs with the net. There was still tons of net left over, so I ran around him again, fastening him to his chair. Mom grabbed my end of the net and tied it securely to hers, and we stood back to admire our work.

"You won't get away with this, you know," Mr. Beeston said, struggling and trying to kick out. All he managed to do was make the chair wobble on its legs.

"I wouldn't do that if I were you," a voice suddenly boomed from the other side of the saloon.

We all turned to see Millie clambering up off the sofa. She stood majestically in the center of the room, arms raised as though waiting for a voice from heaven.

"I put my back out for weeks once, falling backward off a chair. Had to see a chiropractor for six months. And they're not cheap, I can tell you." She swept into the galley. "Okay, who's ready for a nice, hot cup of tea?" she asked. "I'm parched."

The sea had calmed down, and the three of us drank our tea on the front deck. The sky sparkled with dancing colors. As we watched, the lights danced faster and faster. Pink, blue, green, gold—every color you could imagine, in a million different shades, jumping around, stabbing at the water as though it were too hot for them to settle. It seemed as though the lights were speaking—in an alien language that I had no chance of understanding.

Millie looked at them intently for a while, then sniffed her cup of tea. "I don't know what they put in this," she said, draining the cup and heading back inside, "but I'll have to get some."

Mom buttoned up her coat, her eyes fixed on the lights.

"All of this," she whispered. "I remember it all."

"Do you remember my dad?" I asked nervously, recalling what happened last time I had tried to find out about him.

"We never meant it to happen," she said, her eyes misting over. "He told me right from the start how dangerous it would be. It was after the regatta."

"The regatta?"

"We used to hold it every year, but that was the last one. I don't know how we went so wrong, but we did. I went with Mrs. Brig, who used to run the Sea View B & B. She had a little two-person yacht. We got into trouble on the rocks. That was when I met Jake." She looked at me for the first time. "Your father," she added before looking away again. "I don't know what happened to Mrs. Brig. She moved away soon afterward. But Jake and I—well, I couldn't help it. I went back to Rainbow Rocks every night."

"Rainbow Rocks?"

"Well, near enough. I waited by those rocks you took me to. You know?"

"Yes. I know."

She smiled sadly. "You knew more than I did. But not anymore. I remember it all."

"So did he come?"

She shook her head. "I waited every night. Then one night I told myself I'd give it one last try before giving up for good. I just wanted to thank him." She turned to face me again. "He saved my life, Emily."

"And he came?"

She smiled. "He'd been there every night."

"Every night? But you said—"

"He had hidden himself. But he had seen me every time I went. Said he couldn't keep away either, but he couldn't bring himself to talk to me."

"Why not?"

"You know, that first time, when he helped us . . . he never got out of the water." Mom laughed. "I thought at the time, what an amazing swimmer!"

"So you didn't know . . ."

"He thought I'd be shocked, or disgusted or something."

I took a deep breath. "And were you?"

Mom put her hand out to me, cupped my chin. "Emily, when I saw his tail, when I knew what he was—I think that was the moment I fell in love with him."

"Really?"

She smiled. "Really."

"So then what happened?"

"Well, that was when I left home."

"Left home? You mean Nan and Granddad used to live here?"

Mom swallowed hard. "I remember why we argued, now. They wouldn't believe me. They thought I was crazy. They tried to make me see a psychiatrist."

"And you wouldn't."

She shook her head. "So then they sold off everything and moved away from the ocean for good. They gave me an ultimatum—either I came with them, or . . ."

"Or they didn't want to know anything about you." I finished her sentence for her.

"The boat was your granddad's. He didn't want anything more to do with it—or me. Said he'd had enough of the sea to last him a lifetime."

"He gave it to you?"

She nodded. "I like to think the gesture meant that a part of him knew it was true. That he knew I wasn't crazy."

"And what about Jake?"

"I used to sail out to sea to meet him, or around to Rainbow Rocks."

"Was that where they caught him?"

She dabbed the edge of her eye with the palm of her hand. "I never believed it would happen," she said. "Somehow, I thought everything would be all right. Especially after you were born."

"How come they didn't make you move away?"

"Maybe they wanted to keep an eye on us."

"On me, you mean?"

She pulled me close, hugging me tight. "Oh, Emily," she whispered into my hair. "You only saw him once. You were so tiny."

"I'm going to see him again, Mom," I said, my voice coming out in a squeak. "I'm going to find him."

She smiled at me through misty eyes.

"I *am*."

A moment later, I noticed Shona swimming around to the side of the boat. "We're nearly there," she called. "Are you coming in?"

I looked at Mom. "Is it okay?" I asked.

For an answer, she pulled me tighter — then she let me go.

I ran inside and changed into my swimsuit. Millie came back out with me. I perched on the edge of the boat. "See you." I smiled.

Mom swallowed hard and held Millie's hand as I jumped into the water. Within seconds I felt my tail form. My legs melted and stretched, spreading warmth through my whole body. I waved to Mom and Millie as they watched me from the front deck.

"Look!" I shouted, then ducked under the water. I flicked my tail as gracefully as I could, waving it from side to side while I stretched out in a downward handstand. When I came back up, Mom was clapping. "Beautiful," she called, wiping her hand across her eye. She blew me a kiss as I grinned at her. Millie's eyes widened. She shook her head, then picked up Mom's cup of tea and finished that one off, too.

"Are you ready?" Shona asked.

"As ready as I'll ever be," I replied, and we set off.

The Great Mermer Reef isn't like anything you're ever likely to see in your life. It's the highest, widest, longest wall in the world—in the universe, probably —made out of rainbow-colored coral, miles and miles from anywhere, smack in the middle of the sea.

You don't realize what it is at first. It feels like the end of the world, stretching up and down and across, farther than you can see in every direction. I shielded my eyes from the brightness. It reminded me of the school dance we had at our graduation at the end of last year. They'd borrowed a machine that threw disco lights across the room, swirling around and changing color in time to the music. The Great

Mermer Reef was a bit like that, but about a million times bigger and brighter, and the colors swirled and flashed even more.

And somehow, we had to get past it! It was the only way to the prison.

As we got closer, the swirling lights became laser-beam rays, shooting out at every angle from jagged layers of coral heaped upon coral.

Sharp, spiky rocks were piled all the way up to the surface and higher, with soft, rubbery bushes buried in every crevice in the brightest purples and yellows and greens you've ever seen. A moving bush like a silver Christmas tree flapped toward us. Two spotted shrimp dragged a starfish along the seabed. All around us, fish and plants bustled and rustled about. But we were stuck — in a fortress of bubbles and bushes and rocks. We couldn't even climb over the top; it was way too high and rough. Above the water, the coral shot diamond rays where it sparkled with stones like cut glass. I was never, ever going to find him.

"It's hopeless," I said, trying desperately not to cry. It was like that darn game about going on a bear hunt. You keep coming across things that you've got to get past. "We can't get over it; we can't get under it."

Shona was by my side, her eyes bright like the coral. "We'll have to go through it!" she exclaimed, her words gurgling away in multicolored bubbles. "There's bound to be a gap somewhere. Come on." She pulled at my arm and dove deeper.

We weaved in and out of spaghetti-fringed tubes and swam into bushes with tentacles that opened wide enough to swim inside. But it was the same thing every time: a dead end.

I perched on a rock, ready to give up, while Shona scaled the coral, tapping it with her fingers like a builder testing the thickness of a wall. A huge shoal of fish that had been sheltering in a cave suddenly darted out as one, writhing and spinning like a kaleidoscope pattern. I stared, transfixed.

"I think I've found something." Shona's voice jolted me out of my trance. She was scratching at the coral, and I swam closer to see what she'd found.

"Look!" She scrabbled some more. Bits of coral crumbled away like dust in her fingers. She pulled me around and made me look closer. "What can you see?" she asked.

"I can't see anything."

"Look harder."

"What at?"

Shona pushed her face close to mine and pointed into the jagged hole she'd scraped away at. She pushed her fist into it and pulled out some more dust; it floated away, dancing around us as she scraped.

"It's a weak point," she said. "This stuff's millions of years old. I'm sure they have people who check the perimeter and maintain it and stuff, but there's always going to be a bit of it that they miss."

I pushed my own hand into the hole and scrabbled

at it with my fingertips as though I were digging a hole into sand. It felt different from the rest of the wall. Softer. I pushed farther.

Scrabbling and scraping, we'd soon scooped all the way up to our shoulders, white dust clouds billowing around us.

"Now what?" I asked.

"Make it wider. Big enough to swim into."

We worked silently at the hole. The coral didn't glint and glisten with colors once we got inside it. We scraped and scratched in darkness.

Eventually, as my arms were going numb and my whole body was aching and itching from the dust particles swirling all around us, Shona grabbed my arm. I looked up and saw it. The tiniest flicker of light ahead of us.

"We're through," I gasped.

"Nearly. Come on."

Filled with hope, I punched my fist deep into the hole, scratching my hand as I pulled at the wall. The hole grew bigger and rounder, eventually large enough to get through. I turned to Shona.

"Go on. You first," she urged. "You're smaller than me."

I scrunched my arms tightly against my body and flicked my tail gently. Then, scratching my arms and tail on the sides, I slid through the hole.

Once on the other side, I turned and carried on scraping so Shona could get through as well. But nothing came away in my hands. No dust. I cut my fingers against jagged rock.

"I can't make it bigger," I called through the hole.

"Me, neither," Shona replied, her voice echoing inside the dark cavern I'd left behind.

"Try to squeeze through."

Shona's head came close to the hole. "It's my shoulders. I'm too big," she said. "I'll never manage it."

"Should I pull you?"

"I just can't do it." Shona backed away from the gap. "I'll get stuck — and then you won't be able to get back through."

"I can't do it without you." My voice shook as it rippled through the water to her.

"I'll wait here!"

"Promise?"

"Promise. I'll wait at the end of the tunnel."

I took a deep breath. "This is it, then," I said, poking my head into the opening.

"Good luck."

"Yeah." I backed away from the hole again. "And thanks," I added. "For everything. You're the bestest best friend anyone could want."

Shona's eyes shone brighter in the darkness. "*You* are, you mean."

There was *no way* I'd been as good a friend as she had. I didn't tell her that, though — I didn't want her to change her mind!

Then I turned away from the hole. Leaving the Great Mermer Reef behind me, I swam toward a dark maze of caves covered in sharp, jagged pieces of coral.

"I'm going to see my dad," I whispered, trying out the unfamiliar thought, and desperately hoping it could be true.

Chapter Fourteen

J swam cautiously away from the reef, glancing nervously around me as I moved ever closer to the prison. A solitary manta ray slid along the ground, flapping its fins like a cape. Small packs of moody-looking fish with open jaws threaded slowly through the silent darkness, glancing at me as they passed. Ahead of me, a barrel of thick blackness rotated slowly. Then suddenly, it parted! Thousands of tiny fish scattered and reformed into two spinning balls. Beyond them, a dark gray shadow, bigger than me and shaped like a submarine, moved silently between them.

I held my breath as the shark passed by.

As I drew nearer to the prison, the water grew darker. Dodging between rocks and weeds, I finally reached the prison door. It looked like the wide-open mouth of a gigantic whale, with sharp white teeth filling the gap. In front of the door, two creatures silently glided from side to side, slow and mean, with a beady eye on each side of their mallet-shaped heads. Hammerhead sharks.

I'd *never* get past them. Maybe there was another entrance.

I remembered the note in Dad's file. "East Wing," it had said. It was a shame there wasn't one of those *You are here* signs, like you get at the mall.

I figured I'd been heading west since I'd set off from Brightport, because I'd been chasing the setting sun all the way. Shona and I had turned right from the boat to head toward the reef, which meant I should now be facing north.

I turned right again to go east. In front of me was a long tunnel attached to the main cave. It reminded me of those service stations on the highway—the kind on the median that join the two sides together. Apart from the fact that this was made of rock, that is, and it didn't appear to have any windows, and was about fifty feet under the sea. The East Wing?

Swimming carefully from one lump of coral to another and hiding behind every rock I could find, I made it to the tunnel. But there was no entrance. I swam all the way along it, right to the end. Still no opening.

The front gate must be the only way in. I'd come this far for nothing! There was *no way* I'd get past those sharks.

I started to swim back along the other side of the tunnel. Perhaps there'd be a doorway on this side.

But as I made my way along the slimy walls, I heard a swishing noise behind me. The sharks! Without stopping to think, I flicked my tail and zoomed straight down the side so I was underneath the tunnel itself. Pressing myself up against the wall, I wrapped a huge piece of seaweed around my body. Two hammerheads sliced past without stopping, and I inched my way back up again, scaling the edge with my hands and looking around me all the way. A minute later, I noticed something I hadn't seen earlier. There was a gap. I could see an oval shape about half my height and slightly wider than my shoulders with three thick, gray bars running down it. They looked like whalebone. The nearest thing I'd found to a way in — it had to be worth a try.

I tugged at the bars. Rock solid. I tried to swim between them. I could get my head through, but my shoulders were too big to follow. This wasn't going to work.

Unless I swam through on my side. . . .

I tried again, coming at the bars sideways. But it was no good. I couldn't squeeze my face through the gap. I never realized my nose stuck out that much!

I held on to the bars, flicking my tail as I thought. Then it hit me. How could I have been so stupid? I turned to face them. Just like before, I edged my head through the bars, as slowly and carefully as I could. All I needed to do now was flip onto my side and pull the rest of my body through.

But what if I got stuck—my head on one side, my body on the other, caught forever with my neck in these railings?

Before I had time to talk myself out of it, I swiveled my body onto its side. I banged my chin, and my neck rubbed on the bars—but I'd done it! I swished my tail as gently as possible and gradually eased my body through the gap.

I thought back to the time when we were changing to go swimming and how I hadn't wanted anyone to see my skinny body. Maybe being a little sticklike wasn't such a bad thing, after all.

I rubbed my eyes as I got used to the darkness. I'd landed in a tiny round bubble of a room, full of seaweed mops hanging on fish hooks all around me.

I swam to the door and turned a yellow knob. The door creaked open. Which way? The corridor was a long, narrow cave. Closing the door behind me, I noticed a metal plate in the top corner. *NW: N 874.* North Wing? I must have gotten my calculations wrong!

I swam along the silent corridor, passing closed doors on either side. *N 867, N 865*. Each one was the same—a big round plate of metal, like a submarine door; a brass knob below a tiny round window in the center. No glass, just fishbone bars dividing each window into an empty game of tic-tac-toe.

Should I look through one?

As I approached the next door, I swished up to the window and peeked in. A merman with a huge hairy stomach and long black hair in a ponytail swam over to the window. "Can I help you?" he asked, an amused glint in his eye. He had a ship tattooed on his arm; a fat brown tail flickered behind him.

"Sorry!" I flipped myself over and darted away. This was impossible! I wasn't even in the right wing. And there were scary criminals behind those doors! Which was only to be expected, I suppose. This was a prison, after all.

Suddenly, I heard a swooshing noise. Hammerheads! Coming nearer. I flicked my tail as hard as I could and swam to the end of the corridor. I had to get around the bend before they saw me!

With one last push of my tail, I zoomed around the corner—into an identical tunnel.

Identical except for one thing. The numbers all started with *E*. The East Wing!

I swam carefully up to the first door. *E 924*. I tried to remember the number from that note in Mr. Beeston's files. Why hadn't I written it down?

An old merman with a beard and a raggedy limp tail was inside the cell, facing away from me. I moved on. *E 926, E 928.* Would I ever find him?

Just then, two mallet-shaped heads appeared around the corner. I hurled myself up against the next door, frantically twisting the brass knob. To my amazement, it wasn't locked! The door swung open. Banking on the odds that whoever occupied it would be less scary than the sharks, I backed into the room and quietly shut the door. The whooshing noise came past the moment I'd closed it. I leaned my head against the door in relief.

"That was a lucky escape."

Who said that? I swung around to see a merman sitting on the edge of a bed made of seaweed. He was leaning over a small table and seemed to be working on something, his sparkly purple tail flickering gently.

I looked at him, but I didn't move from the door. He appearead to put the end of a piece of thread in his mouth and then tied a knot in the other end.

"Got to keep myself busy somehow," he said somewhat apologetically.

I slunk around the edges of the bubble-shaped room, still keeping my distance. The thread he was sewing with looked as if it was made of gold, with beads of some kind strung on it in rainbow colors.

"You're making a necklace?"

"Bracelet, actually. Got a problem with that?" The

merman looked up for the first time, and I backed away instinctively. *Don't make fun of criminals whose cells you've just barged into,* I told myself. Never a good idea if you're planning to get out again in one piece.

Except he didn't look like a criminal. Not how I usually imagine a criminal to look, anyway. He didn't look mean and hard. And he *was* making jewelry. He had short black hair, kind of wavy, a tiny ring in one ear. A white vest with a blue prison jacket over it. His tail sparkled as much as the bracelet. As I looked at him, he ran his hand through his hair. There was something familiar about the way he did it, although I couldn't think what. I twiddled with my hair as I tried to —

I looked harder at him. As he squinted back at me, I noticed a tiny dimple appear below his left eye.

It couldn't be . . .

The merman put his bracelet down and slithered off his bed. I backed away again as he came toward me. "I'll scream," I said.

He stared at me. I stared back.

"How in the sea did you find me?" he said, in a different kind of voice from earlier. This one sounded like he had molasses blocking up his throat or something.

I looked into his face. Deep brown eyes. My eyes.

"Dad?" a tiny voice squeaked from over the other side of the cell somewhere. It might have been mine.

The merman rubbed his eyes. Then he hit himself

on the side of the head. "I knew it would happen one day," he said, to himself more than me. "No one does time in this place without going a little bit crazy." He turned away from me. "I'm dreaming, that's all."

But then he turned back around. "Pinch me," he said, swimming closer. I recoiled a little.

"Pinch me," he repeated.

I pinched him, and he jumped back. "Youch! I didn't say pull my skin off." He rubbed his arm and looked up at me again. "So you're real?" he said.

I nodded.

He swam in a circle around me. "You're even more beautiful than I'd dreamed," he said. "And I've dreamed about you a lot, I can tell you."

I still couldn't speak.

"I never wanted you to see me in this place." He swam around his cell, quickly putting his jewelry things away. He picked up some magazines off the floor and shoved them into a crack in the wall; he threw a vest under his bed. "No place for a young girl."

Then he swam back and came really close to me; he held his hand up to my face, and I forced myself not to move.

He cradled the side of my face in his palm, stroking my dimple with his thumb, and wiped the tears away as they mingled with the seawater.

"Emily," he whispered at last. It was him. My dad!

A second later, I clutched him as tightly as I could,

and he was holding me in his strong arms. "A mermaid as well," he murmured into my hair.

"Only some of the time," I said.

"Figures."

He loosened his arms and held me away from him. "Where's your mother?" he asked suddenly. "Is she here? Is she all right?" He dropped his arms to his sides. "Has she met someone else?"

I inched closer to him. "Of course she hasn't met anyone else!"

"My Penny." He smiled.

"Penny?"

"My lucky penny. That's what I always called her. Guess it wasn't too accurate in the end." Then he smiled. "But she hasn't forgotten me?"

"Um . . ." How was I supposed to answer that! "She still loves you." Well, she did, didn't she? She must, or she wouldn't have been so upset when she remembered everything. "And she hasn't *really* forgotten you — at least, not anymore."

"Not anymore?"

"Listen, I'll tell you everything." And I did. I told him about the memory drugs and Mr. Beeston and about what had happened when I took Mom to Rainbow Rocks. And about our journey to the Great Mermer Reef.

"So she's here?" he broke in. "She's that close, right now?"

I nodded. He flattened his hair down, spun around in circles, and swam away from me.

"Dad." *Dad! I still couldn't get used to that.* "She's waiting for me. She can't get into the prison." I followed him over to his table. "She can't swim," I added softly.

He burst out laughing as he turned to face me. "Can't swim? What are you talking about? She's the smoothest, sleekest swimmer you could find—excluding mermaids, of course."

My mom? A smooth, sleek swimmer? I laughed.

"I guess that disappeared along with the memory," he said sadly. "We swam all over. She even took scuba lessons so she could join me underwater. We went to that old shipwreck. That's where I proposed, you know."

"She definitely still loves you," I said again, thinking of the poem and even more sure now.

"Yeah." He swam over to the table by his bed. I followed him.

"What's that?" I asked. There was something pinned onto the wall with a fish hook. A poem.

"That's mine," he said miserably.

"'The Forsaken Merman'?" I read. I scanned the lines, not really taking any of it in—until I came to one stanza that made me gasp out loud. *A ceiling of amber, a pavement of pearl.*

"But that's, but that's—"

"Yeah, I know. Soppy old stuff, isn't it?"

"No! I know those lines."

Jake looked up at me. "Have you been to that shipwreck yourself, little 'un?"

175

I nodded. "Shona took me. My friend. She's a mermaid."

"And your mother?"

"No—she doesn't even know *I've* been there."

Jake dropped his head.

"But she knows those lines!" I said.

I pulled the poem off the wall, reading on. "She left lonely forever the kings of the sea," I said out loud.

"That's how it ends," he said.

"But it's not!"

"Not what?"

"That's not how it ends!"

"It does; look here." Jake swam over, took the poem from me. "Those are the last lines."

I snatched it back. "But that's not how *your* story ends! She never left the king of the sea!"

Jake scratched his head. "You've lost me now."

"*The King of the Sea.* That's our boat! That's what it's called."

His eyes went all misty like Mom's had earlier. "So it is, love. I remember when we renamed it. I forget what her father had called it before that. But you see—"

"And she could never leave it! She told me that. And now I know why. Because it's you! She could never leave *you*! You're not the forsaken merman at all!"

Jake laughed. "You really think so?" Then he pulled me close again. He smelled of salt. His chin was bristly against my forehead.

"Look—you'll need to go soon," he said, holding me away from him.

"But I've only just found you!"

"The dinner bell is about to ring, and we need to get you out of here. I don't know how you got your way into this place, little gem, but you sure as sharks don't want to get caught here. Might never get out again."

"Don't you want me?"

He held my hands and looked deep into my eyes, locking us into a world of our own. "I want you alive," he said. "I want you free, and happy. I don't want you slammed up in some stupid place like this for the rest of your life."

"I'll never see you again," I said sadly.

"We'll find a way, little gem." I liked how he called me that. "Come on," he said, looking quickly from side to side. "We need to get you out of here." He opened his door and looked down into the corridor.

"How come you can do that?" I asked. "Aren't you supposed to be locked up in here?"

He pointed to a metal tag stapled to the end of his tail.

"Does that hurt?"

"Keeps me in my place. If I take it across the threshold"—he pointed at the doorway—"and I know what I'm talking about—it's like being slammed between two walls."

"You tried it?"

He rubbed his head as though he'd just bashed it. "Not to be advised, I tell you."

I giggled. "Why *have* doors then?"

He shrugged. "Extra security—they lock 'em at night." He swam back toward me. "You understand, don't you?"

"I think so." I suddenly remembered Mr. Beeston's words, how he said my dad ran off because he didn't want to be saddled with a baby. But Mr. Beeston had lied about *everything*. Hadn't he?

"What is it, little 'un?"

I looked down at my tail, flicking rapidly from side to side. "You didn't leave because . . . It's not that you didn't want me back then?" I said.

"What?" He suddenly swam over to his bed. I'd totally scared him off. I wished I could take the words back.

He reached under the bed. "Look at this." He pulled a pile of plastic papers out. "Take a look. Any of them."

I approached him shyly. "Go on," he urged. "Have a look." He passed me one. It was a poem. I read it aloud.

> *I never thought I'd see the day,*
> *They'd take my bonny bairn away.*
> *I long-ed for her every day.*
> *Alas, she is so far away.*

"Yeah, well, it was an early one," he said, pulling at his ear. "There's better than that in here."

I couldn't take my eyes off the poem. "You . . ."

"Yeah, I know. Jewelery, poetry. What next, eh?"
He made a face.

But before I could say anything else, a bell started
ringing. It sounded like the school fire alarm. I
clapped my hands over my ears.

"That's it. Dinner. They'll be here soon." He
grabbed me. "Emily. You have to go."

"Can I keep it?" I asked.

He folded the poem up and handed it back to me.
Then he held my arms tightly. "I'll find you," he said
roughly. "One day, I promise."

He swirled around, picked up the bracelet from his
bedside table, and quickly tied a knot in it. "Give this
to your mother. Tell her—" He paused. "Just tell her,
no matter what happens, I never stopped loving her,
and I never will. Ever. You hear me?"

I nodded, my throat too clogged up to speak. He
hugged me one last time before swirling around
again. "Hang on." He pulled the poem off his
wall and handed it to me. "Give her this as well, and
tell her—tell her to keep it till we're together again.
Tell her to never forsake me."

"She won't, Dad. Neither of us will. Ever."

"I'll find you," he said again, his voice croaky.
"Now go." He pushed me through the door. "Be
quick. And be careful."

I edged down into the corridor and held his eyes
for a second. "See you, Dad," I whispered. Then he
closed the door and was gone.

I wavered for a moment in the empty corridor.

The bell was still shrieking—it was even louder outside the cell. I covered my ears, flicked my tail, and got moving: back along the corridors, into the cleaning cupboard, through the tiny hole, out across the murky darkness, until I found the tunnel again.

Shona was waiting at the end of it, just like she'd said she would be. We fell into each other's arms and laughed as we hugged each other. "I was so worried," she said. "You were gone ages."

"I found him," I said simply.

"Swishy!" she breathed.

"Tell you all about it on the way. Come on." I was desperate to see Mom. I couldn't wait to see her face when I gave her Dad's presents.

"So tell me again." Mom twirled her new bracelet around and around on her wrist, watching the colors blur and merge, then refocus and change again, while Millie looked on jealously. "What did he say, exactly?"

"Mom, I've told you three times already."

"Just once more, darling. Then that's it."

I sighed. "He says he's always loved you and he always will. And he had stacks of poems that he'd written."

She clutched her poem more tightly. "About me?"

I thought of the one in my pocket. "Well, yeah. Mostly."

Mom smiled in a way I'd never seen before. I laughed. She was acting just like the women in those horrible, gooey romantic films that she loves.

"Mom, we have to see him again," I said.

"He's never stopped loving me, and he never will," she replied dreamily. Millie raised her eyebrows.

A second later, a huge splash took the smile off her face. We ran outside.

"Trying to get one over on me?" It was Mr. Beeston! In the water! How did he get past us? "After everything I've done for you," he called, swimming rapidly away from us as he spoke.

"What are you going to do?" I shouted.

"I warned you," he shouted, paddling backward. "I won't let you get away with it." Then in a quiet voice, his words almost washed away by the waves, he added, "I'm sorry it had to end like this, Mary P. I'll always remember the good times."

And then he turned and swam toward the Great Mermer Reef. Mom and I looked at each other. Good times?

Millie cleared her throat. "It's all my fault," she said quietly.

Mom turned to Millie. "What?"

"I loosened the ropes." Millie pulled her shawl around her. "Only a tiny bit. He said they were hurting."

Mom sighed and shook her head. "All right, don't worry, Millie," she said. "There's nothing we can do now, is there?"

As we watched Mr. Beeston swim off into the distance, Shona appeared in the water below us. "What's up?" she called. "I thought I heard something going on."

"It's Mr. Beeston," I said. "He's gone!"

"Escaped?"

"He went over there." I pointed toward the prison. "I think he's up to something."

"Should we go after him?"

"You girls are not going back there!" Mom said. "Not now. It's too dangerous."

"What, then?" I asked. "How will we get back? We don't have any fuel; the sail's broken. Shona can't tow us all the way back to the harbor."

"We could radio the coast guard," Mom said.

"Mom, the radio's been broken for *years*. You always said you'd get it fixed at some point—"

"But I kept forgetting," Mom finished my sentence with a sigh.

"We could always meditate on it," Millie offered. "See if the answer comes to us."

Mom and I both glared silently at her. Ten seconds later, the decision was taken out of our hands. A loud voice wobbled up from below the surface of the sea. "You are surrounded," it gurgled. "You must give yourselves up. Do not try to resist."

"Who are you?" I shouted. "I'm not afraid of—"

"Emily!" Mom gripped my arm.

The voice spoke again. "You are outnumbered. Do not underestimate the power of Neptune."

Before I could think about what to say next, four mermen in prison-guard uniforms appeared on the surface of the water. Each one had an upside-down octopus on his back. In perfect formation, they leaped from the water, their tails spinning like whirlpools. They flipped on their sides, the octopus legs swirling above their backs like rotary blades, and headed toward us. Between them, they plucked Millie, Mom, and me from the deck, spun themselves around, and held us under their arms as they plopped back into the water.

"I can't swim," Mom yelped.

For an answer, she was dragged silently under the water. Gulping and gasping, we were shoved roughly into a weird tube-thing. My legs started turning into a tail right away—but, for once, I hardly noticed.

We slid along the tube, landing on a bouncy floor. The entrance we'd slipped through instantly closed, leaving us staring at the inside of a white, rubbery bubble. Two masks hung from the ceiling. They looked like the things they show you when you go on a plane.

I grabbed hold of them and helped Mom and Millie put them on. Then we sat in silence as we bumped along through the water. Millie pulled some worry beads out of her pocket and twirled them furiously around her fingers.

Mom clutched my fingers, holding them so tight it hurt.

"We'll be fine," I said, putting my arm around her. Then in an uncertain whisper, I added, "I'm sure we will."

Chapter Fifteen

*T*he good news: they didn't keep us in that tiny, wobbly cage forever. The bad news: they separated us and threw us each into an even tinier one. This time it was more like a box. Five small tail spans from side to side and a bed of seaweed along one edge. It was all Mr. Beeston's fault. How could he have done this to us?

I sat on my bed and counted the limpets on the rocky wall. Then I counted the weeds hanging down from the ceiling. I looked around for something else to count—all I could find were my miserable thoughts. There were plenty of them.

A guard swam in with a bowl of something that looked nothing like food but that I suspected was my dinner.

"What are you going to do with—"

He shoved the bowl into my hands and disappeared without answering.

"It's not fair!" I shouted at the door. "I haven't done anything!"

I examined the contents of the bowl. It looked like snail vomit. Green, slimy trails of rubbery goo spread on top of something flaky and yellow that looked suspiciously like sawdust. Gross. I pushed the bowl away and started counting the seconds. How many of them would I spend in here?

The next thing I knew, I was lying on my side on my horrible bed. Someone was shaking me and I slipped around on the seaweed.

"Mom?" I jumped up. It wasn't Mom. A guard lifted me up by my elbows. "Where are you taking me?" I asked as he clipped a handcuff onto my wrist and fastened the other one onto his own.

But of course he didn't answer. He just pulled me out of the cell and slammed the door behind us.

"Strong, silent type, are you?" I quipped nervously as we swam down long, tunnel-like corridors and around curvy corners then down more long corridors. We soon arrived at a mouthlike entrance with shark teeth across it like the prison door.

The guard knocked twice against one of the teeth, and the jaw opened wider. He pushed me forward.

Once inside, another guard swam toward us. I was attached to a different-but-similar wrist and whisked along a different-but-similar set of corridors.

And then I was thrown into a different-but-similar cell.

Super.

I'd only gotten as far as counting the limpets when they came back for me this time. And this journey took us somewhere different-but-different. *Very* different.

We reached the end of another long corridor. When the guard pushed me through the door, there were no more tunnels. I was looking out at the open ocean again. For a moment, I thought he was setting me free, except I was still attached to his wrist.

The sea grew lighter and warmer. Something was coming into view. Color — and light. Not dancing and jumping around like the Great Mermer Reef, but shimmering and sparkling from the depths of the sea. As we drew closer, the lights emerged into a shape. Like a big house. A huge house! Two marble pillars so tall that they seemed to reach from the seabed to the surface stood on either side of an arched gateway, a golden sea horse on a plinth in front of each pillar. Jewels and crystals glinted all the way across the arch.

"In there." The guard gestured toward the closed doorway, nodding at two mermen stationed on either side. They both had a gold stripe down one side of their tails. As the mermen moved apart, the gates slowly opened.

We swam toward the arch. Long trails of shells dangled from silver threads above us, clinking with the movement of the water.

"What is this place?" I asked as we swam inside. We were in some sort of lobby—the fancy kind they have in really expensive hotels, only even more lavish, and kind of dome-shaped.

Chandeliers made from glasslike crystals hung from the ceiling, splashing mini rainbows around the walls. In the center of the room, a tiny volcano shot out clouds of bright green light—an underwater fountain. The light flowed over the top of the rocky cauldron, bubbling and frothing and turning blue as it melted onto the floor.

"Don't you know anything?" the guard grunted. "This is Neptune's palace." He pushed me forward.

Neptune's palace! What were we doing *here*? I thought about all the things Shona had told me about him. What was he going to do to me? Would he turn me to stone?

We swam across the lobby. Two mermen with long black tails passed us, talking hurriedly as they swam. A mermaid looked up from behind a gold pillar as we came to the back of the lobby. Reaching into his tail, the guard pulled out a card. The mermaid nodded briskly and moved aside. There was a hole in the wall behind her.

"Up there." The guard swam into the hole, pulling me along. Around and around, spiraling upward through tubes, we climbed the upside-down super-slide till we came to a trapdoor. The guard opened it with one push and nudged me through.

We came out into a rectangular room with glass walls. A giant fish tank—except the fish were on the outside! All brightly colored yellows and blues, darting around, looking in as the guard led me to a line of rocks along one edge and told me to sit down. A notice in front of my row had a word written in capital letters: ACCUSED.

Accused? What had I *done*?

In front of me, there were rows of coral seats. Mer-people were loitering here and there, dressed in suits.

One wore a jacket made of gold reeds with a trident on his chest. I watched him flick through files, talking all the time to a mermaid by his side. A merman on the row behind them in a black suit was whispering frantically to a mermaid next to him as he, too, shuffled through files.

At the front, a mermaid facing the court sat at a coral desk examining her nails. Behind her was a low crystal table—and behind that, the most amazing throne: all in gold, the back of the seat tapered upward into three prongs filled with pearls and coral, downward into a solid gold block. The round seat was marble, with blue ripples carved outward from the center to the edges. A golden sea horse stood on either side of the throne: each arm a sea horse body, each leg its tail, stretching downward and curling into a mass of diamonds at its base.

The throne towered over the court—powerful and scary, even when it was empty!

Every now and then, the mermaid in front of the throne rearranged the items on her desk. She had a row of reeds in a line across the top edge, with some plastic papers beside them. On top of these was a sign saying CLERK. A huge pile of files was balanced in one corner. In the other, a grumpy-looking squid sat with its tentacles folded into a complicated knot.

The mermaid kept glancing backward at a gateway behind the throne, which was gold and arched and covered with jewels, like the palace entrance. The gates within it were closed.

A splashing noise opposite me drew my eyes away from the front of the court. Two guards were opening a door in the ceiling; they had someone in between them.

Mom! The guards unhooked a mask from the ceiling, like the ones she and Millie had when we were captured. Mom clumsily strapped it over her face, a tube leading from her mouth up through the top of the box.

She looked around the court with frightened eyes. Then she noticed me and her face brightened a tiny bit. She tried to smile through her mask, and I tried to smile back.

Outside the fish tank, a row of assorted merpeople were taking their seats. A portly mermaid undid a velvety eel from around her neck as she sat down. She made the others all move up so she could make a seat for an enormous jewel-encrusted crab.

Another huddle of merpeople with notebooks and tape recorders chatted to each other as they sat down. Reporters, I guessed. Along the back of the court, a line of sea horses stood in a silent row. They looked like soldiers.

Then a hush fell on the room as a sound of thunder rumbled toward us.

As the noise grew louder, the water started swishing around. The clerk grabbed her table; people reached out to grip the ledges in front of them. *What was happening?* I glanced around as I held on to the coral shelf. No one else looked worried.

The waves grew heavier, the thunder louder, until the gates at the front of the court suddenly opened. A fleet of dolphins washed into the room—a gold chariot behind them, filled with jewels and crystals. The chariot carried a merman into the room. At least seven feet tall, he had a white beard that stretched down to his chest and a tail that looked as if it was studded with diamonds. It shot silver rays across the room as the merman climbed out of the chariot. Sweeping his long tail under him, he slid into the throne. In his hand, a gold trident.

It was Neptune! Right in front of me! In real life!

A sharp rap of the trident on the floor, and the dolphins swiftly left the courtroom, whisking Neptune's chariot away. Another rap and the gates closed behind them. A third, and the water instantly stopped moving. I fell back on my seat, thrown by the sudden calm.

"U-U-P!" a voice bellowed from the front.

Neptune was pointing his trident at me! I jumped back up, praying silently that I hadn't just doubled whatever sentence I was about to get.

He leaned forward to talk to the clerk, gesturing toward me. The clerk looked up at me too, then picked up one of her reeds. Poking the squid with the reed, she wrote something down in black ink. The squid shuffled grumpily on the edge of the desk and refolded its tentacles.

Eventually, Neptune turned back to the courtroom. He stared angrily around. Then, with another rap of his trident, he shouted, "DOWN!"

Everyone took their seats again as the sea horses at the back split into two rows and swam to the front of the court. They formed a line on either side of Neptune.

The merman in the gold jacket stood up. He bowed low.

"APPROACH!" Neptune bellowed.

The merman swam toward him. Then he ducked down and kissed the base of Neptune's tail. "If it please Your Majesty, I would like to outline the prosecution's case," he began, straightening himself up.

Neptune nodded sharply. "On with it!"

"Your Majesty, you see before you a mermaid

and a . . . *human*." He screwed up his face as he said the word, as though it made him feel sick. Pulling at his collar, he continued. "The pair of them have colluded and connived. They have planned and plotted—"

"How DARE you waste my time!" Neptune shouted. He lifted his trident. "FACTS!"

"Directly, Your Majesty, directly." The merman shuffled through a few more files and cleared his throat. "The child before you today has forced an entry into our prison, damaged a section of the Great Mermer Reef in the process—and assaulted one of your own advisers."

"AND? Is there more?" Neptune's face had turned red.

"It's all in here, Your Majesty." The merman handed a file to Neptune, who snatched it and handed it to the clerk without looking at it.

The merman cleared his throat again. "As for the *human*"—he forced the word out—"the same charges apply."

Neptune nodded curtly. "Once again, Mr. Slipreed, will that be ALL?"

"Absolutely, Your Majesty." The merman bowed again as he spoke. "If I could allude to one outstanding area of this case . . ." Neptune clenched his fist around his trident. The merman spoke quickly. "In apprehending the accused, a merchild, acting with the help of another *human*"—he cleared his throat and swallowed loudly—"was discovered in the vicinity."

Millie and Shona! I slapped my hand over my mouth to stop from gasping out loud.

"Both merchild and the other human are being held awaiting instructions from the court."

"From the COURT, Slipreed? ANY old court is that?"

"Your Majesty, they await your divine ruling."

"THANK you, Mr. Slipreed!" Neptune boomed.

"If I may now call upon my first witness . . . Mr. Charles Finright Beeston."

As Mr. Beeston entered the court, I folded my arms. I tried to cross my legs, but remembered they were a tail so I couldn't. He looked different, somehow. As he swam toward Neptune, I realized what it was. I'd never seen him as a merman before!

Mr. Beeston bowed low and kissed Neptune's tail. He avoided looking at me or Mom. "If I may refer to my notes . . ." A line of bubbles escaped from his mouth and floated up through the water as he spoke.

To your lies, you mean, I said to myself.

"Your Majesty, last night I was tricked into a rescue operation involving a yacht and a small motorboat. I was beaten around the head with a boom and tied up while the accused—" He looked quickly at Mom, then at me. Suddenly breaking his flow for a moment, he looked away again and coughed quietly before continuing. "Before they carried out their unlawful plans. Thankfully, the accused were amateurs and not equipped to deal with a high-ranking professional such as myself." He paused and turned toward Neptune.

"BEESTON—do not presume to look to me for compliments! CONTINUE!"

Mr. Beeston's face reddened. "Of course, Your Majesty. And so, I disembarked and sought the strong fin of the law."

"You swam for the guards?"

"Indeed I did, Your Majesty."

"Thank you." Neptune banged his trident on the floor. "DEFENSE!" he bellowed. "Mr. Thinscale? Your first witness?"

The merman in the black suit jumped up. "Thank you, Your Majesty."

I looked around the court, wondering who his first witness was going to be. "Get up," the guard next to me grunted. "You're on." Then he pulled me out of my seat and pointed toward the throne. I swam nervously toward Neptune. Taking my cue from the others, I bent to kiss his diamond-studded tail.

Neptune pulled on his beard and leaned down. "You understand the charges?" he asked in a slightly quieter voice.

"I think so."

"Speak, then!" he snapped. "Do you HAVE anything to say in your defense?"

"Well, I—" I stopped and looked around the courtroom, and at the merpeople watching on all sides. Some were staring at me. Others were talking quietly or laughing—at me, probably. My tail turned to jelly, and I was about to say, "No," when I caught Mom's eyes. She removed her mask for a second and forced herself to smile.

"Do not make me wait," Neptune growled.

That was when I realized what I had to do.

"Um, sir, Mr. —"

"Do I LOOK like a *sir*? A *Mr.*? Do I?"

I flicked my tail a little, propelling myself higher than my three feet eight inches (presuming my tail was as long as my legs — I had never checked), and looked nervously around at the courtroom. "Your Majesty," I corrected myself. "I know this might sound weird, but, well, it's actually kind of nice to be here."

A murmur flickered through the room and along the rows outside it. The reporters scribbled furiously on their pads.

" 'Nice,' did she say?" I heard someone ask.

"Is she being sarcastic?" another one replied.

"It's what I've always wanted," I added quickly. "Not being in court about to get locked up for the rest of my life, obviously. But being here. With all of you. It feels right."

I glanced at Mom. "I mean, I know I'm part human, and my mom's fantastic. She raised me all on her own and everything. But my dad's great, too. Not just because he's a merman, so I get to be part mermaid." I paused and looked Neptune in the eyes. "Although that part's absolutely wicked," I said.

Neptune leaned forward. He scowled, narrowing his eyes at me.

"I mean, it's fantastic—it's swishy! But more than anything, I'm proud of him because of his belief in love." I pulled the poem he'd written out of my pocket and held it out. "My dad might have been locked away, but his feelings weren't."

I glanced at Neptune. A tic was beating in his cheek, a glare shone in his eyes, but his body had softened a little; the grasp on his trident had loosened. "You can't make people stop loving each other just because a law says it's wrong," I said.

The dolled-up mermaid with the pet crab wiped her eel across her cheek. Another took a hanky out of her coat pocket. A few merpeople were nodding. I heard someone at the back say, "She's got a point, you know."

Neptune let out a thunderous sigh and a huge mock yawn.

"My dad fell in love. So what? What did *I* do to deserve to grow up without a father?" I continued.

Tutting noises were spreading through the spectators' seats. A couple of them shook their heads.

"I wanted to see my dad, that's all. Is that so wrong?" I paused and looked at Mom. "If it really is so terrible, if love is such a horrible crime, then fine, lock me up. Lock up my mom, too." I turned back to Neptune. "Your Majesty. That merman"—I pointed to the first one who'd spoken—"he wants us imprisoned because of laws that were written centuries ago. Things have changed. Humans aren't all bad, you know."

As I looked around the courtroom, I paused on Mr. Beeston's face. Neptune remained silent. "Hey, even one of your top advisers had one for a father," I said. Mr. Beeston lowered his eyes as people turned to look at him. "If it can produce such loyal, devoted merfolk as Mr. Beeston, can it really be so wrong?"

I let my question hang in the air for a moment before turning back to Neptune. I couldn't think of anything else to say. "I only wanted to see my dad," I said finally.

Neptune held my eyes for a few seconds. Then he banged his trident on the floor. "I will NOT be told my laws are wrong! How DARE you presume!"

He got up from his throne, banging his trident again. Everyone instantly rose to their tails.

The gates behind him opened. His chariot was waiting outside. "Court will adjourn," he barked as the dolphins swam into the courtroom. Then he leaped into his chariot and swept out of the court.

I slumped back on my rock and waited to hear my fate.

Chapter Sixteen

*N*o one spoke for the first few minutes. Then, gradually, everyone started whispering to each other, like at the doctor's when you have to act like it's a crime to talk. Maybe it was a crime, here. Everything else was, it seemed.

I returned to my seat and looked up nervously to see if I could catch Mom's eye. She was sitting with her head in her hands. Was she mad at me?

We sat like that for ages, the court almost silent while we waited. Some people left; a few took out lunch boxes and munched on seaweed sandwiches.

Then the gates at the front of the court opened. Neptune was coming back in. Everyone leaped up.

Neptune waved us down impatiently with his trident.

He waited for the court to be absolutely silent before he spoke.

"Emily Windsnap." He looked at me and indicated sharply for me to get up. I flicked my tail and stood as straight as possible. He looked at Mom and pointed upward again. "Mary Penelope Windsnap," he read from the card in front of him, and Mom stood up. "You have both defied ME, and MY laws!"

I swallowed hard.

"My kingdom has held by these laws very well for many generations. *I* invent them; *you* abide by them. That's how it works!"

I tried to get used to the idea of living in a cell with a bed of seaweed and limpets on the wall.

"Do you DARE say I am wrong?" he continued, his voice rising with every word. "Do you think you know better than ME? You do NOT!"

He leaned forward to stare at me. What would I get? Ten years? Twenty? Life?

He paused for ages. When he spoke again, a gentleness had fought its way into his voice. He spoke so quietly, I had to hold my breath to hear him.

"However . . ." he said, then stopped. He stroked his beard. "However," he repeated, "you have touched on something today. Something beyond laws." His voice softened even more. "And therefore, beyond punishment."

I held my breath as he paused, tapping the side of his trident.

"You will both be released!" he boomed eventually.

A gasp went through the court, followed by a stream of murmuring. Neptune lifted his trident and glared around the room. The chattering stopped instantly.

"You defied my laws," he went on. "But why? Shall I pretend I do not understand? Or that I have never felt that way? NO! I am no hypocrite! And I shall NOT punish you for love. I shall NOT! Mrs. Windsnap." He turned to Mom. A long deep sigh, his breath rumbling out from his throat. Then— "Your husband is also to be released."

Another gasp whizzed through the court.

"On one condition," he continued. "The three of you will join a community on an island with a secret location. This will be your home from now on. If you break this condition, you will be punished most severely. Do you understand?"

He stared at us both. I nodded vigorously. Had I heard right? Was I *really* going to see my dad again?

The gold-jacketed merman suddenly rose from his seat. "Your Majesty, forgive me," he said, bowing low. "But the other merchild? You know, there could be trouble if—"

"Just get them all out from under my tail," Neptune barked. "She can join them, for all I care. Discuss it with her parents. Either that or a memory wipe."

"Very well, Your Majesty." He sat down again.

Neptune scanned the court. "And perhaps you can all tell your kinfolk that your king is not only a firm ruler, but also a just and compassionate one." His eyes landed on me. "One who will no longer punish folk merely for loving."

Then he got up from his throne and banged his trident on the floor. "Case closed," he bellowed, and left the court.

It all happened so quickly after that. The room erupted in noise. People were clapping and cheering; others gossiped among themselves. A few came over to the dock to shake my hand.

"Can I go now?" I asked the guard. He nodded curtly and pointed to the exit as he undid my handcuffs.

Outside the court, a mermaid with her hair in a bun took my hand. "Your mom will be escorted separately; she'll meet you in a bit," she said. "Let's get you out of here."

"Who are—" I began, but she'd turned around and was pulling me toward a boat that looked like a cross between a limousine and a submarine. It was white and long, with gold handles on the doors.

A crowd was waiting by the limo boat. "Emily, can you tell me how you feel?" one of them asked, a black reed poised above her notebook. I recognized her as one of the reporters from the court.

"Emily doesn't want to talk at the moment," the mermaid said. "She has to —"

"I feel great," I said. "I just can't wait to see my mom and dad together."

"Thanks, Emily." The reporter scribbled furiously as I was bundled into the boat. There was someone else inside.

"Shona!"

"Emily!"

We hugged each other tight.

"We're going to an island!" I said. "My dad's coming!"

"Seat belts," the mermaid instructed from the driver's seat. Then we shot forward like a bullet. As we sped through the water, I told Shona everything that had happened. "And they said you might be able to come, too!" I finished off. I didn't mention the other option. Surely her parents would agree?

"Swishy!" Shona laughed.

"Going up," the mermaid called from the front as we tipped upward, gradually climbing until we came to a standstill. Then she opened a door in the ceiling. "Your stop," she said to me, holding out her hand. I shook it, feeling rather stupid. "Good luck, Emily," she said. "You're a brave girl."

"See you soon," Shona said. She giggled, and we hugged each other before I climbed out. I stood on top of the boat.

Blinking in the daylight, I tried to adjust to the scene. *King* was moored just in front of me. A group of mermen waited in the water in front of it, holding on to two thick ropes. Mom was leaning right over the side, reaching down to someone in the sea. She was holding his hands.

I stood on tiptoe so I could see who it was. For a moment, I thought I must be imagining things. It couldn't have happened this quickly, surely! A mop of black hair, sticking up where it was wet, a pair of deep brown eyes. Then he noticed me, and the dimple below his left eye deepened as he let go of Mom's hands and swam toward me.

"Dad!" Without thinking, I jumped into the sea—and into his arms.

"My little gem," he whispered as he hugged me tight. Then he took my hand and we swam back to the side of the boat together. Mom reached down with both arms and we held each other's hands: a circle, a family.

A second later, a series of splashes and shouting exploded behind us. A bunch of reporters were heading our way.

"Mr. Windsnap." One of them shoved a micro-phone shaped like a huge mushroom in my dad's face. "Simon Watermark, Radio Merwave. Your story has melted Neptune's heart. How does it feel to have made history?"

"Made history?" Dad laughed. "At the moment, my only feelings about history are that I want to go back twelve years and catch up with my wife and daughter."

The reporter turned to Mom. "Mrs. Windsnap, is it true that your baby-sitter helped with your plan?"

That was when I noticed Millie sitting on a plastic chair at the front of the boat. One of the mermen was perched on the deck opposite her, his tail dangling over the side, the pair of them frowning at a pack of tarot cards spread out between them.

"We couldn't have done it without her," Mom said.

The reporter turned to me. "Emily, you were a brave girl to do what you did. You must have had some help along the way. Is there anyone you'd like to say a special thank-you to?"

"Well, I'd like to thank my mom for being so understanding. I'd like to thank my dad for believing in us." He kissed my cheek. "And Millie for falling asleep at the right time."

The reporter laughed.

"And I'd like to thank Shona. My best friend. I could never have done this without her."

But out of the corner of my eye, I saw a familiar figure. Merpeople were talking and laughing in groups all around us, but he was on his own. He looked up and smiled a shaky, crooked smile at me, his head tilted in what looked almost like an apology.

And I forgave him.

Almost.

There was just one thing he could do for me first.

He jumped a little as I swam over to him. I whispered my favor in his ear.

"A mass memory wipe?" he blurted out. "That's ridiculous—not to mention dangerous."

"Please, Mr. Beeston," I begged. "Think about all the nice things I said in there. After everything that's happened, I should hate you forever. But I won't. Not if you do this one little thing for me."

He looked at me hard. What did he see? A girl he'd known all her life? Someone he perhaps cared about, just a tiny little bit?

"Very well," he said eventually. "I'll do it."

I kept my head down as we stood by the side of the pool. Everyone around me chatted in groups. Julia was with Mandy, giggling together in the corner. Fine. I didn't need Julia. I had Shona and no one could be a better best friend than her.

My heart thumped in my ears, blocking out everything else.

Bob arrived. I stepped forward, put my hand up. "Please, sir—I'd like to show you something."

Bob frowned.

"I've been practicing."

He waved a hand out. "All right then," he said with half a smile. "Let's have it."

I stepped toward the edge of the pool.

"Look at *fish girl*," Mandy sneered from the corner. "Showing off again."

"That's right," I said, looking her right in the eyes. "Fish girl is showing off."

I glanced up to the window. Too high. I couldn't see outside, but I knew he'd be there. He promised.

I had five minutes. Five minutes to be proud instead of scared. Five minutes to be free, to be myself. But mostly, I had five minutes to give Mandy Rushton the biggest shock of her life!

And so I dove in. Piercing the surface as gently as I could, I swam underwater all the way to the opposite end of the pool.

"Big deal!" Mandy snorted. "So fish girl can do a length underwater. Whoopdi-do!"

As she mocked me, something was happening under the water. My tail was starting to form. The familiar feeling filled me with confidence. This was it!

I dove straight down. And then I flicked my tail up in the air. Spinning around and around under the water, I could feel my tail swirling and dancing, faster and faster. I couldn't wait to see Mandy's face!

I swam up to the surface, wiped my hair off my face, and looked across. Thirty open mouths. Total silence. If they'd been playing musical statues, it would have been a dead heat.

Mandy was the first to step forward. "But—but—" she sputtered. "But that's a—how did you—"

I laughed. "Hey, guess what, Mandy? I'm not scared of you—and I don't care what you call me. You can't stop me being who I am. And you don't get to bully me anymore, because I'm leaving. I'm off to a desert island, with a whole bunch of—"

A loud rap on the door stopped me saying any more.

Bob walked over to it in a daze. Mr. Beeston. Right on time. He spoke quietly to Bob. "Of course," Bob said, his voice flat and mechanical. "I'd forgotten. Come on in."

He turned to the class. "Folks, we have a visitor today. He's come to give us a special talk."

Mr. Beeston stood in front of the class, a large bag in his hand. "Now then, children," he said. "Listen carefully. I'm going to teach you about lighthouses, and the dangers of the sea."

He opened the bag. "But before we start, let's all have a doughnut. . . ."

I slipped quietly out of the pool as Mr. Beeston held everyone's attention. It was almost as if I'd been forgotten. I would be soon!

"Thank you," I mouthed as I passed behind the class. He nodded solemnly in reply.

I crept away from the pool, changed quickly, and slipped outside. Looking back at the building, I smiled.

"Goodbye, 7C," I whispered. Then I turned and walked away.

We left that night. Mom, Dad, and me, off to a whole new world where who knew what was waiting for us. All I knew for sure was that my life as a mermaid had only just begun.

But remember, it's just between you and me!

ACKNOWLEDGMENTS

Lots of people have helped this book make its way from my computer into your hands. I would especially like to thank:

Mum, for getting rid of all the pounding hearts and lurching stomachs;

Dad, for noticing all sorts of things that everyone else missed;

Peter B., for the title;

Kath, for her eagle-eyed nitpickiness;

Helen, for everything I've learned and gained from working with her at Cornerstones;

Cameron, for lending me books about sea life with great pictures and fantastic facts;

Cath, who hasn't actually had anything to do with the book, but has been a brilliant pal all the time I've been writing it.

With extra special thanks to:

Lee, for an inspirational friendship, and for being so in tune with me and my characters;

Jill, for sharing the journey, and for having endless discussions about mermaids without complaining once;

Catherine, for all her support and guidance, and for finding Emily such a good home;

And Judith and Fiona, for being the perfect editors.

Take a look at Emily's next adventure!

Emily Windsnap and the Monster from the Deep

I swam around my cell for the hundredth time.

"Let me out!" I yelled, scratching my hands down the rocky walls. My voice echoed around me. Finally, I slumped in the corner.

The next thing I knew, the door was rattling. I leaped up as Mr. Beeston came in carrying a net basket filled with shellfish and seaweed. He placed it on a rocky ledge beside me. Water crashed around me as I reached for it, throwing me against the sides.

"See that?" he snarled as I grabbed the ledge to stop myself from being thrown back against the wall. "That's virtually constant now. And it'll keep getting worse, until you've done what you need to do."

I didn't reply.

"Eat your breakfast," he said, nudging a finger at the basket. "You need to be strong."

"I don't have to do what you say." The edges of my eyes stung.

"Really? Well you won't be interested in our new visitor, then. Kyle tells me he's found someone who might make you feel differently."

"A visitor?"

"A friend."

I quickly rubbed my eyes. "You've got her here? But how did you know—"

"Eat up quickly," he growled in a voice that made my skin itch. "It's time for a reunion."

We swam up toward the surface, Mr. Beeston's hand gripping my wrist so tight it burned. The water grew lighter and warmer as we made our way along tunnels and out into clear water. He pulled me down under a clump of rocks, scattering a group of striped triggerfish. A metal gate filled a gap between the rocks.

"Up there," he said.

My heart thudded. I was really going to see Shona! But what if she wouldn't speak to me after everything that had happened? She'd probably hate me even more now, for dragging her into it again. I had to explain. "Can I see her on my own?" I asked.

"What for?"

"It's personal."

"Ah, friendship, so sweet," Mr. Beeston snarled, his throat gurgling into a laugh. He gripped my arm, his broken nails scratching my skin. "You can have five minutes," he said. Then he fiddled with a lock, and the gate bounced open. I swam through it, along a narrow crack. "And don't try anything smart," he called through the bars.

"I won't."

I swam all the way up to the surface. I was inside a cave, in a tiny pool. Gray pillars lined the edges, their reflections somber in the greeny blue water. A tiny shaft of sun lit up the stalactites hanging from the ceiling like frozen strands of spaghetti. Where was she?

I swam between the pillars, where the pool opened out. Slimy brown rocks lay all around. Thick clusters like bunches of candles protruded upward from the water, black as though they'd been singed.

"Shona?" I called.

And then I saw her. Sitting on one of the rocks, her back to me.

But it wasn't Shona.

Her hair was short and black. She turned around. For a moment, she looked shocked. Then she forced her angular face into a twisted smile.

"Hi there, fish girl," she said. There was a smug look on her face, but I was pretty sure her voice wobbled a little. "Long time no see."